Judith Kerr's
CREATURES

Judith Kerr's
CREATURES

My Manx husband always referred to his parents
as his creatures, so this title includes not only
much-loved animals but also a much-loved family.

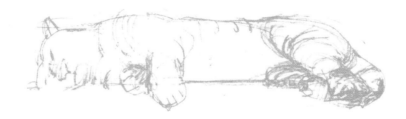

HarperCollins *Children's Books*

For my children and grandchildren.

Frontispiece: Mother, Father, Michael and me, 1928
Opposite: our house in Berlin
Page 6: the same, by me aged 6 or 7

The Acknowledgements on page 176 constitute an extension of
these copyright notices

First published in hardback in Great Britain by HarperCollins
Children's Books in 2013.
10 9 8 7 6 5 4 3
ISBN: 978-0-00-751321-5
HarperCollins Children's Books is a division of HarperCollins
Publishers Ltd.
Text and illustrations copyright © Kerr-Kneale Productions Ltd 2013
The author/illustrator asserts the moral right to be identified as the
author/illustrator of the work.
A CIP catalogue record for this title is available from the British Library.
Visit our website at: www.harpercollins.co.uk
Printed and bound in China

Contents

1

Germany, Switzerland and France

THERE ARE DRAWINGS and there are illustrations. I first discovered the difference aged four and a half at my German kindergarten. Up to that point I had had no problems. I had successfully hopped up and down on one leg, sung little German songs and constructed a salt cellar out of cardboard. But then one day the kindergarten fräulein plonked a flower down in the middle of the table and said, "Today we are all going to draw a tulip."

I looked at the tulip. There seemed to be a lot of curved bits, which I did not yet know were called petals, so I drew one. But when I looked up from my drawing it no longer looked the same. It had shifted side-ways and looked narrower, so I changed it and drew the one next to it, and then another and another and another. But each time I looked up they shifted again and I was trying to remember which ones I had drawn and which were still to do, when the kindergarten fräulein appeared beside me. "What on earth are you doing?" she said. "Don't you know how we draw a tulip? *This* is how we draw a tulip."

I could see at once that hers was better than mine. Anyone could see that she had drawn a tulip. And yet, I thought, when I had looked at it, it had seemed quite different… I didn't draw from life again for the next twelve years, until I went to art school.

I can't remember a time when I didn't want to draw. It seemed a normal way to pass one's time, just as it was normal for my brother Michael to kick a ball about. I liked to draw figures in motion, and I always drew them from the feet up, which I would now find difficult. No one else in my Jewish family drew. My mother composed music and my father was famous throughout Germany for his writings about the theatre and his travels, and for his witty verse in which, among other subjects, he mocked and reviled Hitler and the rising Nazi Party.

I think I always felt that my drawing concerned no one other than myself and stubbornly ignored well-meant advice from grown-ups. Only once someone – I think it was a visitor – mentioned almost in passing that when you looked at the real world you did not actually see a large blank space between the ground and the sky. I had got rather good at positioning my running and playing children on a strip of green crayon at the bottom of the paper with a strip of blue crayon at the top, but when I checked I found to my irritation that he was right, and started, reluctantly at first, to add bits of background and the beginnings of perspective.

My mother was very proud of my drawing and carefully preserved my better efforts. I still find it very moving that when we had to flee Germany early in 1933, she packed these pictures among the things she thought most important to save. I was then nine years old and had been totally unaware of what was happening around me in Berlin. My first realisation came when my sixty-five year old father, who had been in bed with 'flu, disappeared overnight and my mother explained to Michael and me that he had fled the country.

What happened to my family then, and later as I grew up, is the story I told in my three novels, collectively entitled *Out of the Hitler Time*. However, they *are* novels, in the sense that they are selective, certain events have been dramatised and others reduced. As the story is told from the point of view of Anna (someone approximately like myself), it automatically cannot include any information that was not available to Anna at the time. There are also facts about what happened to my parents which I did not know even at the time of writing the books, but which have only gradually emerged over the years. Forty years later, the following account is not a novel, but an attempt to tell the facts.

My father had been warned that there was a plan to take away his passport and, in spite of his illness, had caught the first train out of Germany. My mother, brother and I followed by a roundabout route, after a tense delay during which we had to keep my father's absence and our own imminent departure a secret. My father's fear was that if our plans were known, the Nazis might keep us as hostages to get

him back. We reached Zurich, where he was anxiously waiting for us, a few days before the elections which gave Hitler complete power. Afterwards we heard that on the following morning the Nazis had come to our house to demand all our passports.

The first thing to happen after we had safely reached Switzerland was that I became horribly ill. For a month I had a high fever, life threatening in those days before antibiotics, and can remember little about it. During that month my parents' lives began to fall apart. They had never been wealthy, but my father had had a regular income from his journalism (he was also co-editor of the *Berliner Tageblatt*, a newspaper similar to the London *Times*) and from his books, which were widely read. From the moment the Nazis came to power all payments to him were stopped. Eventually he managed to pay our hotel and the doctors' bills by getting a friend to sell a boxful of first editions from the depot in Berlin where my mother had stored our possessions. But soon afterwards all the rest was confiscated. My father's writings were publicly burned and he was deprived of his German nationality. A few months later the Nazis offered a reward to anyone who captured him dead or alive.

And yet, through all this, my parents managed to make my brother and me feel that it was all a great adventure. As soon as I had recovered from my illness, we went to live in a lakeside inn near Zurich, and it was exciting to go to a Swiss village school, to learn the local dialect and the local customs, and to draw these slightly different looking people. My father's work was well known in Switzerland and he had expected to be able to write there, much as he had in Germany. However the Swiss, in spite of their professed

neutrality, were depressingly eager to keep in with Hitler, and he suddenly found it difficult to be published. So, as he also spoke and wrote perfect French, by the end of 1933 we moved to Paris. There my parents took a small furnished flat high up in a building not far from the Arc de Triomphe and my brother and I started at French schools. At first it was difficult, but at the age of ten it is not all that hard to learn a language, and once one has done it, it gives one a terrific boost. I loved the brief clarity of French as opposed to the long convolutions of German and was inspired, towards the end of our stay in France, to write an eighty-page French story about some children heroically averting a train crash. However, when I try to read it now, I find that I have forgotten the meaning of some of the words. The French school day is very long, and I don't remember doing very many drawings, but I must have done some, because I remember, (a) a great row because I had spilt some of my Indian ink on the floor of the flat, for which we might be made liable, and (b) an art teacher at one of my schools who invited me to her studio to help me draw details like hands, which I was very bad at. But, as always, I refused – gracefully, I hope.

The cover and illustrations for Pierre et Michelle, *1935*

By the summer of 1935 Michael and I had become quite settled in France. We both came top in French in the final exams, as, I have since discovered, did a lot of other refugee children: something to do with appreciating a language when one can compare it with another, perhaps. My mother had learned to cook French dishes, which were much nicer than anything we had ever eaten in Germany and I loved being in Paris – so much so that one evening when my father and I were looking out over the Paris rooftops at the lights below, I'm told I said, "Isn't it lovely being a refugee!"

The irony of this must have struck him, for my parents were in fact facing another financial crisis. My father's work in France had been mainly for the *Pariser Tageblatt*, a German newspaper for refugees. As the refugees had very little money, the paper didn't have much either. My father earned only small sums and they were often late. Occasionally he was asked to write something for a French newspaper, but 1935 was the height of the Great Depression. Even French writers were out of work, so these occasions were rare. In a desperate attempt to earn some money, he had written a film script – something he had never done before. It was promptly turned down by various French film companies, so he had sent it to England, but had heard nothing more.

Pierre et Michelle

par

Anna Judith Herr

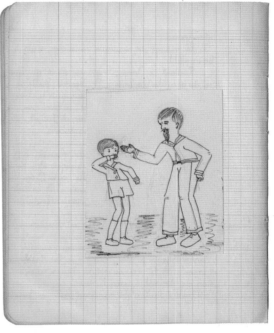

When school finished for the summer my parents gave up the Paris flat and we went to stay in a Belgian seaside hotel for a holiday and to wait, I suppose, for a reply. There was a wide beach, the weather was lovely, Michael and I swam, flew a kite and built large complicated sand castles, and thought it was great. It was only when the weather turned colder and the other guests gradually all left, but we were still there, that we began to realise something was not right. At last my parents called a family meeting and explained to us that they had decided to travel to England to see if we could start a new life there, and that in the meantime we were to stay with our maternal grandparents who had a flat in the south of France.

14

*Angels, some wingless because
I couldn't draw wings in perspective*

Dutch dancing

"Il me faudrait au moins cinq chouffleurs comme ça pour mes petits-enfants!"

16

Wir gehen auf die Reise

We all travelled back to Paris together, and there they put us on a train to Nice, while they waited in a cheap railway hotel for the meeting of a charitable refugee organisation, which would eventually lend them enough money to go to England. Later my mother told me that they sat there for three weeks, and she survived only by reading the whole of *The Forsyte Saga*, which she said kept her sane, but probably didn't give her the most accurate picture of the England in which she hoped to settle.

It couldn't have been easy for my father to make the decision to send us to our grandparents. I had no idea at the time that they never spoke to each other. This was because, many years before in Berlin, my grandfather, who, in spite of being married to my grandmother, always went in for a lot of ladies on the side, had put money into a play on condition that one of these ladies, an aspiring actress, should star in it. My father was known for being totally incorruptible – so much so that, even though he loved actors, he refused always to meet them socially, lest this might interfere with his criticisms.

This page and bottom left: illustrations of our stay in Nice

"Euer grässlicher Opapa hat mich wieder eingeschlossen!"

Hippolyte est malade !!!

Monsieur et Madame Raisin n'ont qu'un seul enfant: Hippolyte, le petit ange. Il est charmant, ce petit (Au moins d'après l'avis de ses parents): Toujours sage – lorsqu'il dort, – toujours content – lorsqu'il a tout ce qu'il demandait, – toujours propre – lorsqu'on vient de le baigner. –

Et puis, il est énormément doué pour la musique: Voilà seulement deux ans qu'il a pris des leçons avec un pianiste célèbre, et il sait déjà près-

Silence !

Votre professeur, un grand homme vigoureux avec (hélas) de très bons poumons, engueule sa classe: "C'est a-bo-mi-nable! C'est trop! J'en ai assez! Je vous reporterai à Monsieur le Directeur. Vous aurez 100 lignes! 200 lignes! 300 lignes! Il sera retenu, ce garçon insupportable! impoli! indiscipliné! Cet enfant stupide! Ce phénomène de

This page and opposite: compositions written in England, but still mostly in French

18

A Fir-tree, a Lady-bird
and a Toad-stool

"Yes," said the lady-bird, "isn't it
a simply horrid summer?" The
lady-bird was sitting on a
toad-stool.
"Horrid?" asked the toad-stool.
"Horrid??? It's a lovely, beautiful,
splendid, nice and wet summer."
"Wet!" said the fir-tree. "It certainly is wet. But it certainly is
not a nice summer. Why, I am
dripping wet, and simply can't

So he reviewed the play and wrote that this lady no doubt had many talents, but that acting was not one of them – whereupon my grandfather (who, incidentally, was Secretary of State for Prussia at the time) hired two thugs to beat him up. When my father was walking in the Berlin woods a day or two later they accosted him, but their hearts were not in it, and the three of them ended up having a beer together. My father described this encounter in his column the following week. One can see that, after this, conversation between my grandparents and my father would have been difficult.

I don't think Michael and I were unhappy in Nice. We both went to school. We had arrived after the beginning of the school year and the only girls' school that still had places was one in the port area. My grandmother horrified me with the suggestion that she should teach me sewing and embroidery at home instead of sending me to this rough place, but eventually relented, and of course it was fine. I think some of the older girls used to hang about the nearby barracks after school and the classes were very large, but the lessons were the same as in all French schools. I remember sitting at the back, peering through the mist from the Mediterranean, which somehow crept in even through closed windows, to see what I could of a scientific experiment being conducted on the teacher's desk. Later I wrote triumphantly to my parents, "I am now learning chemistry!"

Of course we both missed them. Our stay in Nice was always referred to as purely temporary, but we had finally understood the financial situation, and sometimes secretly wondered whether our parents would ever have enough money to have us back. But then, just when it was getting rather worrying, it all came right. There was a letter from my parents to say that my father's film script had been bought for £1,000. They both came to collect us. My mother was wearing a new dress. My father and my grandparents exchanged a few awkward words, and then my parents, Michael and I set off on the two-day journey to London. We arrived in early March 1936, almost exactly three years after leaving Berlin.

Drawings, 1938

2

London and the War

I F ONE CAN SPEAK German and French, it is not very hard to learn English, and my brother and I already had a smattering. He had studied it at school, and I, with help from the dictionary and my grandmother, had worked my way through something called, I think, *The Madcap of the Fifth Form* by Angela Brazil, from the Nice English Library. (I later caused a certain amount of surprise when I referred to things as "ripping" and "topping".) Even so, at first I found speech confusing in England and I remember that for a while it was difficult to communicate with anyone outside my family, because I would start a sentence in English, then perhaps go into French and then into German.

My parents used a slice of the £1,000 to send Michael to a minor public school. This turned out to be a brilliant investment, as he was immediately a huge success both at games and at work – so much so that when, inevitably, a term or two later we could no longer afford the fees, the school loaded him with scholarships, so that there was nothing to pay. He then won a major scholarship to Cambridge and then another scholarship to study law and he ended up as a judge at the Court of Appeal.

In the meantime I went each day to a house in Campden Hill Square, to share lessons with two American girls who were being educated at home. It was a very relaxed way of learning a language. The girls and I became great friends, and their parents were infinitely good to me. Later, when, inevitably, we had again run out of money and could no longer afford to pay for my room in the shabby Bloomsbury hotel where we were living, they let me stay in their home, until the war grew threatening and they were advised by their government to return to America.

I am not sure why my parents chose to live in a hotel rather than a flat as in Paris. Perhaps it started as a temporary measure. Perhaps my mother was not ready at first to start on another round of cooking and housekeeping. Perhaps my father still hoped to be able to go back to France, where he could speak the language. While my mother spoke almost perfect English, my father's English was limited. For a writer this must have been terribly hard. I think they had great hopes of my father's film script, which never materialised. It had been bought by Alexander Korda, a Hungarian who, almost single-handed, had created a thriving English film industry. But the film was never made, and we have sometimes wondered whether he ever intended to make it or whether he just wanted to help. Either way he saved our lives by bringing us to England, since otherwise the Germans would certainly have caught us in Paris in 1940.

The drawings I made in London during this time are nearly all black and white. I don't think this was for aesthetic reasons, but rather because hotel rooms and messy paints don't mix. In 1938 several kind ladies paid for me to be sent to a fashionable, rather snobbish girls' boarding school. It was done with the best possible intentions but, unlike my brother, I did not shine at games – my final report read, "Judith has learned to cradle her crosse at last" – and my cheap clothes and my American English accompanied by French gestures did not go down well. Since such great efforts had been made to send me to the school, I could not very well admit this, and my letters home were all about how happy I was. I made friends in the end, especially with Lavinia Thorpe, Jeremy Thorpe's sister. I always remember that when her parents came to take us both out to tea, she insisted that we go to the cheap village teashop, which was all my parents could afford, rather than the country house hotel they usually frequented because, she said, it was much nicer. We even edited a terrible rebel magazine together, and I successfully passed my school certificate. But when we were singing 'Jerusalem' on our last day of school and everyone else was in tears, I was the only one who didn't cry. I have to admit to a certain satisfaction when after the

Pen drawings, 1937

HOTEL FOYER SUISSE

(Managed by "Schweizer Verband Volksdienst.")

12, BEDFORD WAY,
LONDON, W.C. 1.

Telephone :
Management : MUSeum 2982
Visitors : MUSeum 2251

Telegrams :
Inland : Foysuisse Westcent London
Foreign: Foysuisse London

Quatorze Juin, Mille neuf cent quarante.
J'ai dix-sept ans aujourd'hui.
L'age où l'on est toujours contente,
L'age de bonheur, sans soucis.

Ce jour même, le sort se décide,
et Paris a capitulé.
Hitler est aux Invalides,
Gestapo dans les Champs Elysées.

Tuileries, Montmartre, Madeleine,
Tout est envahi par les Huns,
et au lieu des jolies Parisiennes
On ne voit que des uniformes bruns

J'ai dix-sept aujourd'hui.
Mais ce jour de ma naissance
est le jour de la mort de Paris.
Est-ce la mort, aussi, de la France?

Poem about the fall of Paris. My father must have written my name at the bottom of it.

war the place was turned into the headquarters of the Communist Electrical Union.

I left at sixteen just before the outbreak of war and at the beginning of 1940 began a foundation art course at the London Polytechnic. This I did like. The emphasis was on design and simple techniques and I realised for the first time what an awful lot I didn't know, which was sobering, but also exciting. But money was again a problem and after a term I had to get a job. By this time, anyway, the real war had started. Paris fell, the Germans had reached Calais, the invasion of England was expected any moment and nothing seemed to matter very much, since it looked extremely unlikely that one would survive. In the panic, Michael had been interned on the Isle of Man, and my

parents both had suicide pills. Not being able to study drawing was hardly the most urgent problem.

As Hitler advanced across Europe, our hotel filled up with refugees from the various countries he had overrun. They all congregated in the lounge, where there was a radio, to listen to the nine-o-clock news. This was the time of what was later known as the Battle of Britain and one waited tensely for the figures – so many of our planes shot down, so many of theirs. I remember the night when the number of German planes shot down was said to be 182. The number was later amended, but even so, at the time everyone knew that it was the breakthrough. It was incredible. For the first time one thought that perhaps... perhaps, after all, one might live through this. Then came the Blitz and, like everyone in London, we spent our nights in the cellar and were sometimes very frightened, and like so many others we were eventually bombed out. But then the weather grew too bad for the bombers and the invasion hadn't happened. There was hope.

I think it was during those dark months in 1940 that I became a Brit. Up to then my contact with the English had been mostly with the girls at my boarding school – hardly a representative sample. Now for the first time I saw the patience and humour of the ordinary people as, after terrifying sleepless nights, they struggled to work through the broken streets. And their tolerance: though my parents both spoke with unmistakable German accents, no one ever said anything nasty to them. And their kindness: I remember one instance in particular. Being German but anti-Hitler we were officially categorised neither as "Enemy Aliens" nor as "Friendly Aliens", but as "Friendly Enemy Aliens". (This *Alice in Wonderland* term alone seems to me almost enough reason to want to be British.) Friendly Enemy Aliens were allowed to move from their address but had to report to the police in advance.

Once, when the Blitz was at its worst, I had been offered a few nights' rest in the country, but I didn't want to go because, with all communications being constantly disrupted, I was afraid my parents might be killed in a raid, and I wouldn't even know about it. I was still arguing with my mother at the police station, when one of the policemen said, "It's all right, Miss, you go to the country. I'll keep an eye out for your parents. Police telephone lines are always repaired immediately, and I promise you that if anything should happen to your parents I will ring you up." This is the sort of thing that stays with one.

My brother's internment was eventually resolved through a letter from my parents to Michael Foot, then a journalist, who passed it

A rather heartless Christmas card I sent my brother when he was a pilot in the RAF

It don't mean a thing if you don't pull that string!

on to the government. This was when the Blitz was at its height and people must have had other things on their minds, but my brother was released within days. He taught at his old school for a year and then managed to become one of the few German pilots in the RAF.

After we were bombed out we moved to Putney. Unlike Bloomsbury, where the railway stations were always a target, the bombers were not interested in Putney.

I became a firewatcher and turned out at night whenever there was an air-raid warning, but nothing happened except that I got chilblains. I believe that the only time an incendiary dropped, there was a bitter quarrel as to who would be allowed to put it out.

By this time I had also got a job. I had hoped to work for one of the ministries, but they were closed to anyone not British born. So I became a secretary to a kind, charitable lady called The Hon. Mrs Gamage. She was a colonel in the Red Cross and helped the war effort in various ways from her offices in the bombed-out Children's Hospital in Vincent Square. My job was to look after the knitters all over the country to whom we sent wool, which they knitted up into various garments for the Forces and which we then passed on to anyone in need. The relatives of officers who had been killed also sent us their kit to pass on. (Officers, unlike ordinary men, had to pay for their own uniforms.) And then there were the local ladies who came in every day to make hospital pyjamas and bandages, and who had to be given Bovril in the morning and tea in the afternoon. I suppose it was useful but it was hardly demanding. However, I was so thrilled to be at last financially independent, paying my hotel bill every week and no one having to worry about me, that for a while I was perfectly happy.

Here I must explain something about my family's finances. As a writer who had lost his language, it had become more and more difficult for my father to support us all in England. For a while he had still been able to write for the *Pariser Tageblatt* from London, but even this had stopped with the fall of France. In 1938 the friends who had sent me to boarding school also found a job for my mother as social secretary to an immensely wealthy lady called Lady Wimborne, which I think she quite enjoyed, but when this came to an end, she had to take more and more dreary secretarial work. (She had taught herself to type, but when taking dictation had to rely on her excellent memory, as she couldn't do shorthand.) It was not always easy to get these jobs and, frantic with worry, she would talk endlessly about her efforts – that someone still had not answered her letter; that someone else still hadn't rung back. We knew every detail.

Right: Shelterers, 1943

I did not know that all this time my father, too, was battling to earn money for his family because he never spoke about it. I still did not know it when I wrote *Bombs on Aunt Dainty* in 1973, and I describe my mother as making all the efforts while my father, while writing beautiful words, remained fairly inactive. I now know that this is totally wrong.

Much has happened in the past forty years. First of all, my father's books have been republished in Germany. He is again loved and revered. But, perhaps equally important, there is now an archive in Berlin which holds vast amounts of correspondence – letters to him and from him – which I had never seen. Here is a letter from him to Einstein, on having been offered a speaking tour of America, asking if he would use his influence so that his family could be included. (Einstein tried and failed, and my father did not go.) Here a letter to someone at Oxford, offering to lecture on German Drama. Here are endless suggestions to the BBC German propaganda department, often witty verses about something in the news that morning, and which he had personally delivered to the BBC the same afternoon. (They were rarely used. The reason given was that his views were so well known in Germany that they would have little effect.) He never stopped. And I wish I had known more of all this when I wrote *Bombs on Aunt Dainty*. But at least I am putting it straight now.

Anyway, back to 1941. I think it was in the spring of that year that the art schools first thought again about evening classes. In fact the first one was not an evening class at all – there was still too much danger from air raids after dark – it was a life class held on Sundays at St Martin's School of Art. It cost very little. I could afford it from my earnings, and so I went. I remember it was a cold, bright day. I sat with the drawing board propped up in front of me and looked at the tired, naked woman reclining on

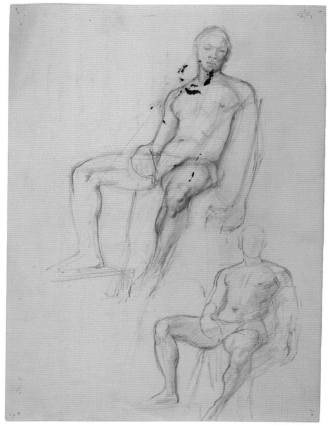

This page and opposite: life drawings

28

a bit of drapery in front of me, and realised that I had absolutely no idea what to do next. But I had to do something, so I began to draw. The only things I remember about that first attempt at a life drawing was a sort of knotted nest of fingers – she must have folded her hands – and a desperate detailed attempt at her permed hair.

It was so awful that I had to go back. Gradually I got some help and advice from the various instructors. I began to realise that all those years when I had thought I was drawing, there had been this vast hinterland of drawing from life, which I had always rejected, but on which everything else depended. It became essential to master it.

The man who taught me most was John Farleigh. He was an illustrator and painter who had had a great success not long before with a book called *The Black Girl in Search of God* by George Bernard Shaw, which he had decorated with beautifully designed woodcuts. He had a passion for drawing and a great urge to pass this on. His female students tended to fall in love with him (I was no exception) and he did not discourage them. By today's standards these relationships were very chaste and limited mostly to the odd kiss behind the paint cupboard. One day, talking to my friend Peggy Fortnum (who later did the original illustrations for *Paddington Bear*), we discovered that we had both been involved with him in this innocent way at much the same time. But we consoled ourselves with the thought that he did seem to pick only the more talented students. He remained a very good friend to us both.

As the nights grew calmer, the Sunday class was replaced by evening classes at the Central School of Arts and Crafts, and I enrolled first in one, then another and then in them all. My job finished at half past five and I just had time to walk to Westminster and catch one of the trams with yellow tinted windows which trundled along the Embankment, in time for the six o'clock life class. My days became a preparation for the evenings and the drawings gradually got better. In time there was also a painting class. I acquired canvases, oil paints and a succession of sketch books, and spent my lunch hour drawing. I even made a sale. A man sitting next to me in a Lyons tea shop offered to buy a sketch "for the price of a lunch," he said. He clearly didn't eat much, for he only gave me half a crown. Still, it was a triumph. Later I managed to talk the owner of a restaurant in Victoria Street into letting me decorate his restaurant. It was made up of several interconnecting rooms, so there were a lot of walls and I painted murals on all of them, somehow incorporating various mirrors which he insisted on keeping. I was quite pleased with the result. But when I went back to see them after the war he had painted all the walls cream with a wallpaper frieze of delphiniums along the top. "Better like this, isn't it?" he said. The mirrors were still in place.

Above: early painting class

Opposite: overnight train travellers, 1947

D-Day came, then the frightening V1 flying bombs, which Londoners called Doodlebugs, and the terrifying V2 rockets, which exploded without warning and laid vast areas waste. Knowing that it was nearly the end, one was more desperate than ever to stay alive. But then, at last, it was over. On VE Day I went out into the crowds. There were people dancing, paper flags being waved, children riding on their parents' shoulders, and a sort of happy hum of chatter and laughter – nothing triumphant, nothing organised, just people who could at last relax, who knew, at last, that they had survived. I thought, this is the country for me. I had brought my sketchbook and drew everything in sight, for hours. Unfortunately that sketchbook, along with a number of others, has disappeared, probably during one of our moves. Every so often I search our attic in the hope that they might be hidden in some corner, but they are gone and I still mourn them.

With the war over, I was desperate to go to art school full time, but as always money was a problem. John Farleigh tried to find a scholarship which would pay me enough to do a proper art course without having to have a job, but they were all for British born only. Finally he found something called a trade scholarship, which he thought would not be limited in this way. It meant having a job connected with drawing two days a week and being paid enough to go to art school the other three days. I managed to get a job in the studio of a textile manufacturer, though I didn't really know anything about textiles. Then, on Farleigh's recommendation, I took my portfolio to see a man at what was then called the LCC, the London County Council. I watched him as he looked through it all. At the end he said, "This is very good, but I'm afraid this scholarship too is only for British born." Then he said, "But let's see how we can get round this."

A few weeks later I got a letter to tell me that I had got the scholarship. I shall never forget him.

3

Art School and After

IT WAS ONE OF THE CONDITIONS of my scholarship that I should study a trade at the Central, but in those gloriously unbureaucratic times it was easy to get round it. Farleigh said, "You don't want to do textile design, do you? Why don't you do illustration?" I said all I wanted to do was draw and paint from life, so he suggested that I sign on for the illustration class every morning and then go wherever I liked. And that's what I did for three years.

The job was all right too, after a slightly dangerous moment at the beginning.

The company that employed me produced furnishing fabrics. They bought in designs in one colour combination, and it was my job to design four or five different colourways, so that anyone who liked the pattern could buy it in the combination they preferred. I had no difficulty with the colours, but I couldn't work out how to get the repeating pattern perfectly aligned. I remember struggling with this at the end of my first day, and the boss coming in and looking dubious, so I mumbled something about finishing it in the morning and raced to the Central for quick instructions. I managed to produce a correct piece of work next day.

Left: textile design Village Wedding

Oil painting of witches, 1948

It was extraordinary being able to do nothing but draw and paint all day. As I knew nothing whatever about textiles, even the two days a week spent on the job were interesting at first, and I made up for the time I missed at the Central by going to evening classes. By this time I had made up my mind that I wanted to be a painter and we were wonderfully lucky in the people who taught us. Apart from John Farleigh there were Bernard Meninsky, Ruskin Spear and Morris Kestelman. It was wonderful.

Things were more difficult at home for my parents. My father was finally earning more money, though in a rather strange way. Having been largely rebuffed by the BBC German Department, he was asked by the Spanish Department to write pieces in French, which were then translated into Spanish and broadcast to South America. But my mother found it more and more difficult to get one of the secretarial jobs she hated but desperately needed.

Before we became refugees, my mother had composed two operas. The first had been briefly performed in a minor opera house, and I

remember being taken to see it when I was five. However, for her
second opera my father had written the libretto. It was a story about
a time machine invented by Einstein, whom they both knew – in fact
my mother, meeting him at a party, had once asked him to explain his
theory of relativity to her. (She said she totally understood it at the
time, only couldn't quite remember it afterwards.)

The libretto was very witty and entertaining. My mother had
almost finished composing the music and had had great hopes of it,
when Hitler came to power and we had to leave Germany. I think
that later my parents showed it to various people here and in France,
but no one was interested. So she gave up composing, but always
thought of what might have been. This, combined with the endless
worry about money, made her very unhappy. But at the start of 1947
she was lucky at last. The American Occupying Force in Germany took
her on as translator, which meant going back to Germany, but with
the American Army and earning dollars. It completely solved all our
financial problems, and she was excited at the prospect of the adventure.

However, it left my father alone. Also, as my mother and I had shared a room, which I could no longer afford on my own, I had to move into digs close by. But my mother and I agreed that I would go and see my father every evening when I got back from the Central.

"Bonsoir, papa". Das Glück tritt in mein Zimmer,
    Ein leises Leuchten hat mein Herz erhellt.
Dein Auge lacht;ein leichter,lustiger,lustiger
    Liegt auf der Welt.

Im Irrsal dieses irren Erdenballes
    Ging doch das eine Labsal nicht zugrund:
"Bonsoir,papa" - das lieb' ich über alles
    In Deinem Mund.

Und,süsse Puppi,dieses ist mein Wille:
    Bald bin ich fern,den ewigen Schatten nah -
Ruf es noch einmal in die grosse Stille:
    "Bonsoir,papa..."

My father's poem
about my evening visits

38

I did not find this a burden. The evening class finished at eight o'clock, so I got back about nine and usually found my father sitting at his typewriter in his shabby room ready to talk. Now that I was able to do nothing but draw and paint at last, I was overwhelmed with thoughts and ideas and I wanted to talk about them all. The only problem was that I did not know all the words I needed in German, and he did not know them in English. In the end we communicated in a mixture of English, German, French and a certain amount of telepathy, but it was totally successful.

People often ask me what my father wrote and it is difficult to answer, because I am always conscious of my limited German. He was passionate about the theatre and very witty, so, like Bernard Levin, he was read even by people who had no prospect of ever seeing the plays he was reviewing. But he also loved to travel and to look at the world, and wrote about it in beautiful lyrical prose and verse, which is untranslatable. He was a perfectionist, and when I redraw something for the umpteenth time, I take comfort from the fact that he corrected his writings not only after they had been published, but even after they had been burned by the Nazis. Perhaps this is also the time to say that all through the years of our emigration he never stopped writing and that most of this has now been published in Germany. Like all our family, he became a naturalised British subject in 1947. For this one needed several respectable people to sponsor one. John Farleigh was one of mine. One of his was George Bernard Shaw.

Left: my mother on her honeymoon in Venice
Overleaf: The Spiritualists, *1946*

Textiles: below, scarf design, and bottom Jeux d'enfants
Opposite: Spring

42

Textiles: left and top, Circus

Above: Little Jungle

Overleaf: Victoria

That summer, with friends from the Central, I went abroad. We took the boat to Calais and then travelled to Basle overnight by train. It took twelve hours. The seats in our third-class compartment were bare wood and very narrow and it was difficult to sleep, so after a while I gave up and spent the night drawing everyone else. We spent a week or so in the mountains and then went to Paris which was a little shabby, but otherwise unchanged. I remember mainly hours spent looking at the Impressionists, and a café where every night we would dine regally off two fried eggs – a banquet if one was used to English rationing.

My textile firm expanded, and I was able to recruit my friends. Peggy Fortnum introduced us to various sentimental Victorian songs, which we used to sing at the top of our voices while we did the fairly undemanding work. I started designing textiles in my spare time and managed to sell the occasional one, but most of my time was spent painting. During my last year at the Central I had a painting accepted by the Royal Academy and another one by the prestigious London Group, and I also won a painting prize at the Central.

Bottom: oil painting, Three Old Women, *shown at the London Group, reviewed, right Opposite and above:* Ghosts, *ink and crayon*

large landscape, " Clover Fields near Top[?]/field Church," an impressive painting in which the design has been very completely worked out while at the same time the observation of a particular effect of light is almost as fresh and sharp as in a sketch.

Mr. Allan Walton's " Labourer's Cottage " admirably conveys the character of a real place, Mr. Ruskin Spear's interior with figures, " Harry's Café," is a work of brilliant observation, Mr. William Gear's abstraction, "Woman Seated," has some real originality of colour, Miss Judith Kerr's " Three Old Women " has a good deal of vitality, the colour of Mr. P. Potworowski's " The Reading Girl " is extremely seductive, Mr. Julian Trevelyan's " Rue de l'Ouest " is one of the liveliest and most entertaining of this artist's recent works, Mr. Graham Sutherland's " Landscape with Rocks " has a fine richness of colour, Mr. H. E. du Plessis uses his elegant calligraphy to great advantage in " The Bookcase," and Mr. Blair Hughes Stanton's " Water Meadows, near Stratford St. Mary " is a candid, gentle, and attractive landscape. Other works to be noticed are Mr. Quentin Bell's lively head in plaster of Mr. Desmond McCarthy, Mr. Robert Hurdles's soundly composed " Camberwell: The Surrey Canal," Mr. Charles Ginner's characteristic landscape " The Kitto Rock, Boscastle," and Mr. Kenneth Martin's " Interior with Figure," which makes a skilful use of glowing colour.

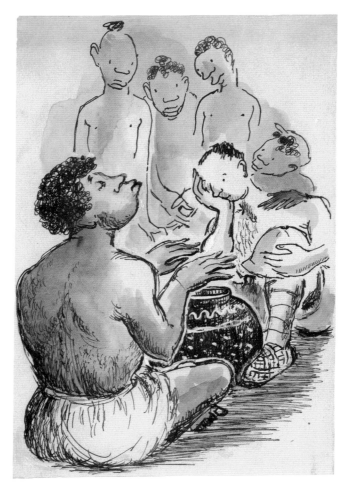

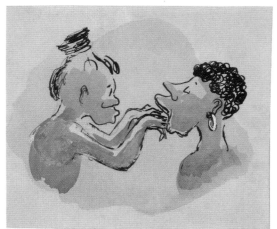

50

However, suddenly during my last term it was decided that all students must be assessed for a diploma at the end of their course, and that this would include a show of work and an essay about their subject. Since I was officially studying illustration, I tried frantically to produce some, but of course it was much too late and, anyway, my heart wasn't in it. In my essay I claimed rather tactlessly that really there was no such thing as illustration as a separate branch of art – look at Picasso who had just done beautiful illustrations for Buffon's *Histoire Naturelle*. Needless to say, I failed. It was ridiculous, and I shouldn't have minded, but I did.

Then, in October, my father had a stroke. He had flown to Hamburg in a troop plane at the behest of the British Control Commission who wanted him to write about the German theatre, as he had done in the past, to raise German morale. When he arrived, he was given a tremendous reception. There were journalists and photographers at the airport, he was given a great lunch, and when he entered the theatre that night, the audience stood up and applauded. He watched a not very good performance of *Romeo and Juliet*, and then at night in his hotel room he collapsed.

A German journalist found him in the morning. He was lying on the floor, partially paralysed, but he knew what had happened and he could speak. He said, "I've had a stroke. But it was not the performance. It was bad, but not *that* bad."

His condition did not improve, and some weeks later, with the help of my mother, he took some pills which ended his life. Sixty-five years later I can still have a conversation with him in my head.

By this time my brother had finished at Cambridge with a double first and had come to London to study law, so he and Ronnie, another lawyer, and I shared a furnished flat in Notting Hill. I ditched the

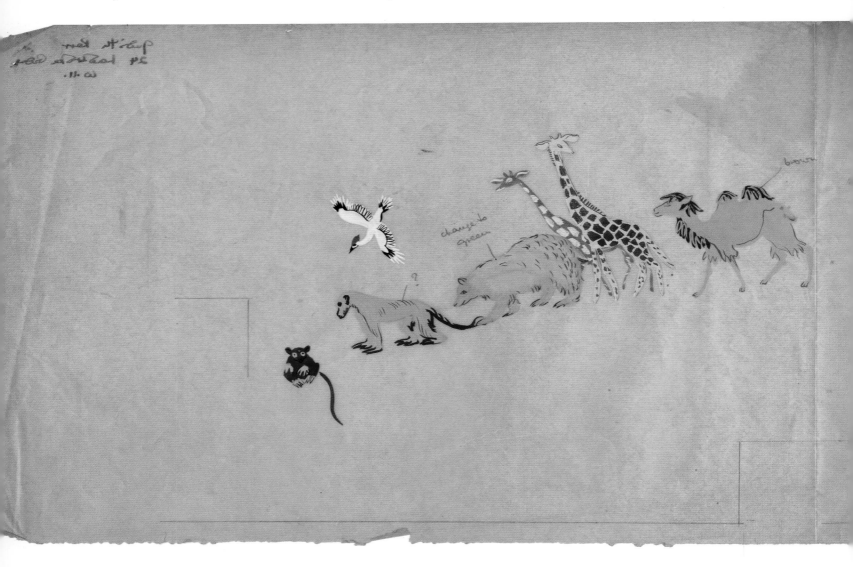

textile studio for a job teaching art at a girls' school in Eastbourne. It was a small school, so, by catching a very early train, it was possible to teach all the classes in one day, and quite often there were people to draw on the journey. I also continued to sell the odd textile design and I got a few commissions to decorate the walls of friends' nurseries.

This brought in enough to pay the rent, especially as I was let off half a crown a week by the two boys in exchange for doing the cooking – rather a miserly reduction, but on the other hand I couldn't cook. Michael probably knew what he was in for, but, looking back, I do feel that Ronnie, who had spent four years in a Japanese prisoner-of-war camp, deserved better. However, he was very forgiving, and became a lifelong friend to us all.

The flat was of course without heating, and the furniture was so rotten that most of it soon collapsed. We were afraid that we would be charged for it if we threw it out, so we stored it on the huge water tank for the whole house, which was in our bathroom, and when one took a bath, one was threatened by this great pile of broken tables and chairs looming perilously above.

Below: sketch for nursery decoration

Sketch for nursery mural decoration on 2 walls. Scale $\frac{1}{7}$.

For each of us it was our first taste of complete independence and very exciting. However, after the intensity of the three years at the Central, it was also a little lonely.

I took on a further teaching job, this time a couple of evening art classes with children from the Paddington slums. All they wanted was to attend a dance session, but in order to do this they had first to sit through an hour of either art or hygiene. I always felt that hygiene might have been more useful, as I kept catching things from them, but I got very fond of them, and briefly considered chucking everything to help them properly. But I don't suppose I would have been very good at it.

Then I had a bit of luck. In 1949 Lady Rothermere, who was involved with the Daily Mail Ideal Home Exhibition, decided to devote a small part of it to paintings by young artists, and a painting I had based on one of my train drawings won first prize. It was worth £100 and so I was able to travel to Spain with two ex-army types who had the use of an old car. We were camping, and as the car would not

Opposite: the squared-up composition for the prize-winning painting. The photograph shows Lady Rothermere, the painting and me

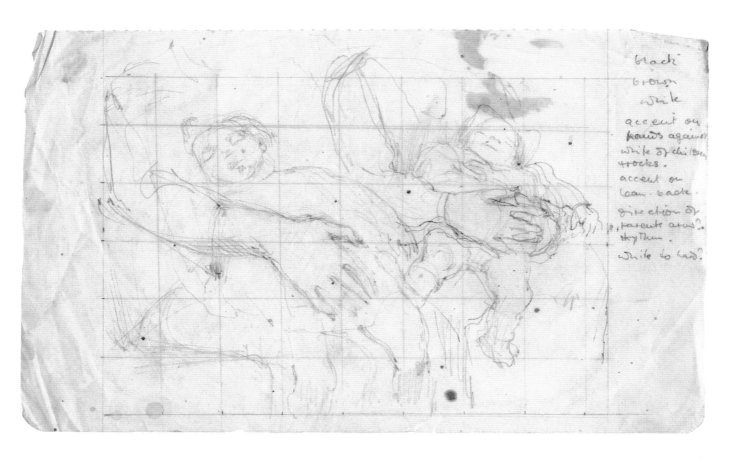

Textile: Spain

start in the mornings without being pushed, we always had to camp on top of a hill, which was apt to be chilly. But it was wonderful to see first France and then Spain unroll as we, rather slowly, made our way south, and later I based a textile design on what I had seen. In the Prado I remember climbing to a totally deserted bright, hot room at the top, where the walls were covered with drawings by Goya.

In 1951 I was able to give up the job in Eastbourne, because an ex-fellow student from the Central passed on her London teaching job to me. This was in a girls' technical school which had a junior art course, as well as courses for cooks, upholstresses etc. It was an excellent school. Even though some of the girls were not at all academic, they were rightly full of confidence because they knew they were good at their chosen trade, and I have always been sorry that technical schools were later abandoned along with the grammar schools. I taught all the girls, not only the ones on the art course, but there was a problem with the cooks, who were supposed to design beautiful decorations in icing sugar. Only of course there was no icing sugar, so they had to draw the sort of designs they would have made out of icing sugar if there had been any, which was not very satisfactory.

The school was in Lime Grove, across the road from the BBC Television Studios. A few of the girls had access to a television set either at home or, more often, at the home of someone in their street, and in the morning at school they would talk about what they had seen. Everyone was curious about this new invention, and when a woman I met at a friend's house told me that she worked at the Television Studios and invited me to lunch there, I leapt at the chance. And this was the best decision I ever made, because, as we ate our lunch in the crowded canteen, Tom Kneale sat down at our table.

4

Tom and the BBC

TOM, WHOSE PROFESSIONAL NAME was Nigel Kneale, was a
29-year-old Manxman. While I was studying art at the Central,
he had studied acting at RADA and had gone on to carry
spears at Stratford. However, he had also been publishing short
stories since he was twenty, and they had been collected in a volume
called *Tomato Cain*, which had won the Somerset Maugham Award.
He was fascinated by this new medium of television and was then
employed by the BBC as a sort of dogsbody scriptwriter, which meant
doing everything from adapting stage plays to writing dialogue for
some vegetable puppets which had been abandoned by their creator.
(They were voiced by most of the Carry On team and he himself
played the onion.) When I met him, the BBC had just stopped paying
him out of the petty cash and had given him some sort of a contract.

I can't remember what we talked about at that lunch, only that
afterwards he walked me back to the bus stop, and a few days later
we went to the theatre and saw a play that was so bad that we were
both in stitches, and then we had a Chinese meal, and at the end of
the evening, going our different ways on the tube, we both thought
that we would probably get married.

Not long after this I was told that, instead of the two days a week
I had been teaching at the technical school, I would have to teach
full time, which would leave me no time for my own work, and Tom
suggested that, rather than teach, I apply for a job at the BBC. They
were looking for someone to read and report on unsolicited plays sent

in by the public, and, probably because I could read plays in other languages, they gave me a three months' trial. I used to collect the manuscripts, read them at home, and bring them back the following week. They were nearly all terrible rubbish, but the BBC, because of their Public Service status, were under an obligation to react to each one. With a lot of help and advice from Tom, I learned how to sum up the contents – I remember that a totally disproportionate number were set in heaven – and at the end of the three months I got the job.

Then came the Coronation. It gave television an enormous boost. Suddenly everyone wanted to watch it at home on their own nine-inch set. BBC drama expanded and the plays got more ambitious. In 1953 Tom was asked by Michael Barry, the head of Drama, to write a six-part serial. Tom suggested science fiction, as a total change from the very limited stagey productions which were the norm, and was teamed up with Rudy Cartier, an Austrian ex-film director who was as eager as Tom to break out.

I recently found a diary Tom kept at that time. He wrote the first episode in a week. The second episode took him four days, and he wrote the third episode over one weekend. After that it got more complicated because he had to go out with Rudy to film some scenes to be inserted later. The serial was called *The Quatermass Experiment*, and the first episode went out – live, of course – while he was still writing the last. They were broadcast from primitive studios at Alexandra Palace, on ancient cameras which were fixed to the floor and which showed the picture upside down and right side to left.

It was all done on a shoestring, and Tom's script was vastly more complicated than anything that had ever been done before so we all helped as much as possible.

Tom with the creature from Quatermass and the Pit

The story was of a rocket being launched into space. (This was eight years before anyone had succeeded in doing this.) It goes up with three men in it and comes back with them mysteriously merged into one. And with something else alien, invisible. What then happens is set in the everyday London of the time, as the alien, in the form of strange vegetation, grows and gradually takes over.

There was a scene towards the end where the vegetation has invaded Westminster Abbey. When Tom discussed this with the unfortunate set designer, Tom claims that the designer said, "You wrote it – you do it!" So Tom bought a tourist guide to Westminster Abbey, cut out a photograph of Poets' Corner and had it vastly enlarged. It was then mounted on board with a slot cut at the top. For the next two days, I sat with two washleather gloves on my hands, while Tom covered them with all sorts of tendrils and twirls of wire, leather and threads.

Tom with Rudy Cartier

When the episode was broadcast he stood on a box behind the picture of Poets' Corner and poked his fingers with the twirly bits through the slot. Then, at the right moment, he very, very gently moved his fingers. And the entire nation was terrified.

The first episode caused a stir. The second episode emptied the streets and the pubs, and by the time the third episode went out, we knew that something extraordinary had happened. I remember coming out of Alexandra Palace, and as we began to walk downhill to the tube station, we looked at the television aerials dotted all over London below us, and we knew that every single one had been watching. It was television drama's first huge smash hit. Even now, sixty years later, people still remember it.

At first we didn't know what it meant. We went off on holiday to Italy, travelling all over the country, and ended up in Berlin where my mother was working, to tell her that we were getting married. When we got back, the BBC were busy comparing offers from film companies (though unfortunately they did not consider that Tom was entitled to any of the money), and everyone wanted Tom to write for them.

In the following years he wrote two more *Quatermass* serials, both filmed, though I still prefer the television versions, happily preserved

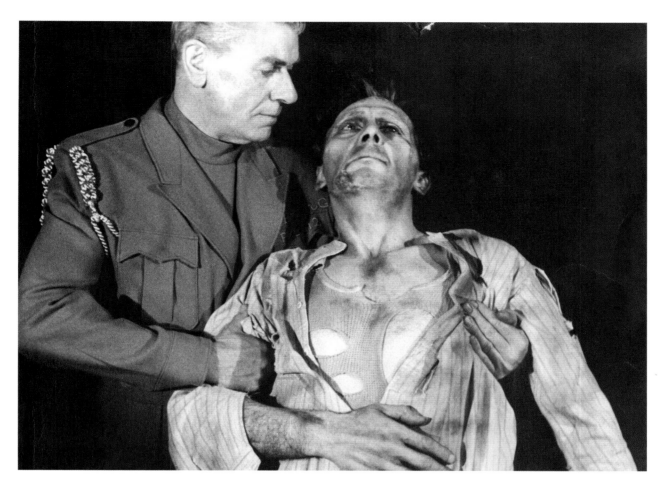

on DVD. Also *The Abominable Snowman*, a play about the yeti, which was also filmed, and an adaptation of Orwell's *1984* (then still largely unknown to the general public) which caused such a furore that questions were asked about it in Parliament.

About this time I was offered a full-time job as reader, which meant that I would be writing reports on plays submitted by proper authors, with an office in the BBC's new Television Centre in Wood Lane. This was very tempting. My part-time job during the previous year had left me plenty of time to paint, but I had not achieved nearly as much as I had hoped. And I had met Tom's brother Bryan, who was seven years younger than I was, and light years ahead of me as a painter. When Tom had won the Somerset Maugham Award, Bryan had won the prestigious Rome Prize. (He is now one of the most highly regarded sculptors in the country.) My paintings – and I hadn't even produced very many of them – suddenly seemed very small beer. And on the other hand, here was something interesting and new, and some quite clever people thought I'd be good at it. So I said yes and moved into Tom's world of actors and writers and dramas and rehearsals, and loved it, though I sometimes felt a bit guilty, as though I'd betrayed something.

Above: still from 1984 *with Peter Cushing and André Morell*

Below: Bryan Kneale with one of his sculptures, later displayed in the forecourt for the RA Summer Exhibition, 2009

We were married in 1954. Tom's parents came from the Isle of Man and my mother from Berlin. Rudy said he would take the wedding pictures, but his camera went wrong, and none of them came out, so we have just one, taken by a newspaper photographer. We found a tiny flat. Though food rationing was still in force, for the first time since the war you could buy furnishings in bright colours, and we had a wonderful time fitting it out.

And so began an extraordinarily happy four years with both of us working in television at a time when it was more exciting than at any time before or since. There was very little management, no committees, no advisory bodies. Just the writer, the producer (who was also the director), his assistant and the cast, and they were all totally involved. The script was written and usually very soon afterwards it went into rehearsal. It was broadcast, live, and there was an immediate reaction. In that sense it was like the theatre, but with an audience not of hundreds, but thousands. And you were among your peers. I remember once, after working late, sitting with Tom in the pub we all used, when the legendary Tony Hancock and Sidney James walked in after a brilliant show. We had all seen it, and, though no one said anything, a great wave of love and admiration went out to them, and they knew it.

Right: wedding, 1954

62

In 1955 a script unit was formed under the leadership of Donald Wilson, who later wrote the hugely popular television version of Galsworthy's *Forsyte Saga*. Television had expanded so fast that there was a shortage of people who were familiar with working in it, and he came up with the idea that I could become a writer. So I was sent on a course (an essential at the BBC before any change of job) and I became first a script editor and then a scriptwriter. I was not at all sure that I could do this, but the people in charge seemed to take it in their stride. I suppose they felt it wasn't much of a risk, as, if I made a total mess of things, Tom would put them right. Their main concern was that I shouldn't use my married name for fear that it would look like nepotism. So I used my maiden name Kerr. Unfortunately they had forgotten that there was already another member of the script unit called George Kerr. So, as everyone knew, anyway, that I was married to Tom, it was generally assumed that in addition to this I was also George's sister.

At first being a scriptwriter meant writing the odd scene to extend a stage play and attending rehearsals in case of any problems. I had seen so much of this with Tom, and simply by talking with him about his work I had learned so much, that, though I found it difficult at first, I could manage it without too much trouble. But then it was decided that I should write a six-part serial – an adaptation of John Buchan's *Huntingtower*.

Left and opposite: stills from **Huntingtower** *with James Hayter, Richard Wordsworth and Leo Maguire*

This is when it hit me. What was I doing, I thought, trying to write a three-hour television serial when English wasn't my first language? And with Scots dialect, too.

Was one really allowed to write in a language which one had only spoken since the age of twelve? If I had grown up in Germany and had been asked to write a German script in a Saxon dialect, wouldn't I have automatically known how to do it? (Which was nonsense, of course.) In the end I agreed with Donald that I would write it in plain English and that, since he was a Scot, he would add the Scottish touches. But it was still terribly difficult.

What made it even more difficult was that soon after starting work on it I had a miscarriage, which was followed, as it so often is, with a depression. With advice from Tom I had written quite a good first episode, but after this I remember sitting for hours and days, as it seemed, unable to think of anything at all. The second and third episodes took forever. I was given whatever happiness pills were current at the time, but they had an unexpected effect. Having always been totally silent at the weekly script meetings, I found myself one day making a long and rather belligerent speech. However, everyone was very patient, eventually the fourth and fifth episodes came more easily, and at long last I happily finished the script. And a few weeks later I discovered that I was pregnant again.

Huntingtower went out in the summer of 1957, embellished with bits of Scottishness by Donald, and with an excellent cast, and was an outstanding success. It was exhilarating. I thought, perhaps I really am a writer. Learning to draw and living as a painter had been such a battle, whereas writing had been almost thrust upon me by people who thought it would be a good idea for me to do it. I immediately set about dramatising a wonderfully subtle short story by Katherine Mansfield, but the result was plonking and dreadful, and the BBC rightly refused to have anything to do with it.

After this I more or less concentrated on being pregnant. The BBC was always very protective when any of their staff became pregnant, and not much was demanded of me. I translated a play from the French and adapted it for television, and Stuart Burge decided to put it on just before my baby was due, which meant that I sat in the tiny production suite with Stuart and the technicians during rehearsals, and any suggestions I made were immediately agreed for fear that I might give birth on the spot.

When I finally left I was given a special payment of £100 – normal policy, they said, for any BBC employees leaving to have a baby. Tom had also been awarded a special payment for writing "a programme of unusual interest", i.e. *The Quatermass Experiment*. But this was only worth £50.

Two weeks after I left, Tacy was born by emergency Caesarean, carried out by a surgeon still in his dinner jacket, rushed to the hospital from a party. One of the people congratulating me on the birth wrote, "Your life will never be the same again." I wasn't at all sure that I liked this. I had liked my life as it was. But of course it was true. It became totally different. And in retrospect, richer and better.

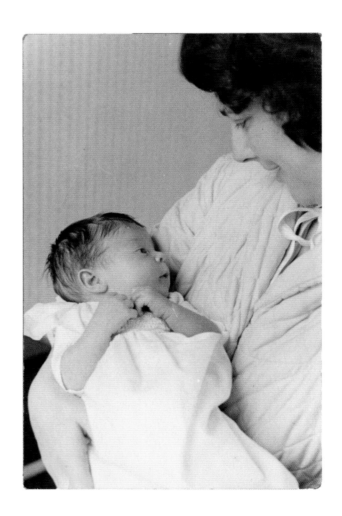

5

The Children and the Books

I HAD ALWAYS TAKEN IT FOR GRANTED that I would look after my children myself, so we never had a nanny or an au pair. Like most new mothers, I found it difficult at first, and of course I missed the excitement and drama of the television studios. But shortly before Tacy's birth Tom had decided to go freelance, so the three of us were at home, juggling his typewriter and the baby about our tiny flat. When the juggling became too difficult we found a bigger flat nearby. Its walls were painted a nauseous sea green, so we pushed the pram round there each day to paint them white, with Tacy watching from her playpen in the middle of the room. When we went home again it was dark, and Tacy would stand at the front of her pram like the captain of a ship gazing intently at the night and the lights. She loved being out in the dark, and later I remembered this.

Once we had moved I used to put her out in the pram on fine days, rushing to look out of our second floor window every few minutes to make sure that she was still there, and I remember watching her as she looked at the pictures in a cheap rag book that someone had given her. She was looking at the pictures with total, rapt concentration – far more than any grown-up looking at pictures in a gallery – and it did occur to me that she ought to have something better to look at than the ill-drawn pictures of a toothbrush or a washcloth in the book.

Tom was very busy at this time. He was writing the screenplays first for John Osborne's *Look Back in Anger* and then for *The Entertainer*,

Left: Tacy, born in 1958 and, above, three years later with her brother Matthew

which starred Laurence Olivier. He was out a lot of the time with Tony Richardson who directed both films. Tacy and I amused ourselves as best we could, but sometimes it did get rather boring. She was determined always to have my full attention and if, while rearranging her toy animals to her design for the fourth time or fifth time, I tried sneakily to think about something else – possibly even some work I might do – she would say severely, "What you thoughting, Mummy? Stop thoughting."

She loved stories, and Tom and I both made them up for her, and of course we also went to the library, but the books for two-year-olds were disappointing. There seemed to be very little between the "here is a cow and here is a horse" kind and some long and not particularly interesting stories with a lot of unfamiliar words "to enrich your child's vocabulary," they claimed. They had to be translated into simple (and sometimes better) words that Tacy knew, and by the time I had done that, the potatoes I was cooking for supper had probably boiled dry. It seemed extraordinary that there were so few books with proper stories in simple words which a two-year-old could understand.

Quite often we went to the zoo. In those days before David Attenborough it was the only way you could see the animals. Tacy was suitably amazed at the sight of all these extraordinary creatures and she especially liked the tigers. We used to stand and gaze at them. However much you thought you knew what they looked like, they were always even better – even sleeker, even more dramatically striped, even a brighter orange. After these visits I used to make up stories about the animals, and one she liked was about a tiger. This was at a time when Tom was out filming again, which left us a bit lonely. By the time we had been for a walk and had tea and exhausted all possible permutations of the toy animals, we both wished that something would happen, that perhaps someone would come to see us. So I made up a story about a tiger coming to tea. She preferred this to all the other stories (some of which, I thought were perfectly good) and would say imperiously, "Talk the tiger." The story was gradually edited and refined, until it was exactly as she liked it, and in the end I had told it to her so often that I knew it by heart.

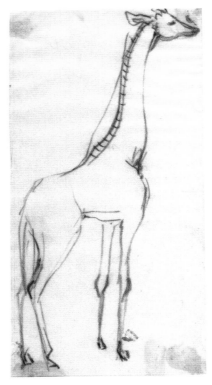

Matthew was born in 1960. Suddenly the flat was again too small, and we moved again, this time into a house in Barnes. Matthew also liked the story of the tiger, but I always felt he had reservations, possibly because he felt he could make up better stories himself. His toy animals all had adventures which he sometimes told us about. There was one especially, called Roger the Badger, whose nightly doings put *Quatermass* in the shade.

And then, suddenly, after seven years of my being Mum twenty-four hours a day, they were both at school every day till three o'clock

Big City *rough*

and I was free to do some work. But what? I did not want to go back to television with its dramas and deadlines, and I had of course never quite stopped drawing, even when I was at the BBC. There had been some attempts at a kind of romantic vision of a big city which never got beyond a rough, and I had done drawings to amuse the children, and sketched them. But it seems extraordinary to me now that for about twelve years of my life I did not do any serious drawing, and I sometimes wonder how much better at it I might be if I hadn't spent so much time doing other things.

In the end I thought I would try to make the story of the tiger that both children had liked into a picture book. At least, I thought, it was reasonably short, and none of the words would need to be translated. I had no idea where to start, and for the first time regretted all those illustration classes I had always avoided. Watercolour seemed the obvious medium to use, but I was not comfortable with it. Just then an old friend from the Central dropped in. His name was Brian Davis, but later, under the name of Michael ffolkes he became a brilliant cartoonist and ended up running *Punch*. At that time he was experimenting with painting and he gave me a very good picture of a head he had painted using indelible inks – wonderful, he said, because you could layer them and achieve a richness which nothing else would give you. So I bought some inks and tried various tiger colours layered in yellows and orange, and they were exactly right.

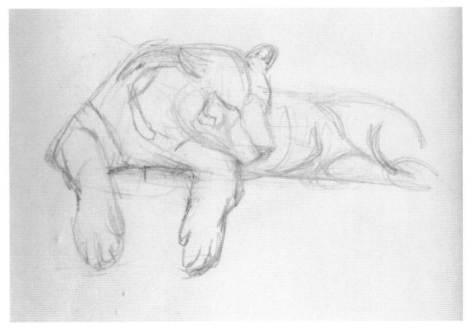

Opposite and above:
zoo sketches

Then I went to the zoo to draw tigers. It seemed simplest to base the family in the book on Tom, Tacy and myself and to give them our kitchen, and then I just plunged in. I got a lot of it wrong at the first go, so it needed redrawing, and the children caught measles, and had holidays and dentists' appointments and tea parties, so it took me the best part of a year to get to the end. Then, even though I knew it wasn't perfect, I thought I'd better show it to someone, so a few weeks before Christmas 1966 I took it to Tom's literary agents who, kindly, I thought, said they would show it to Collins.

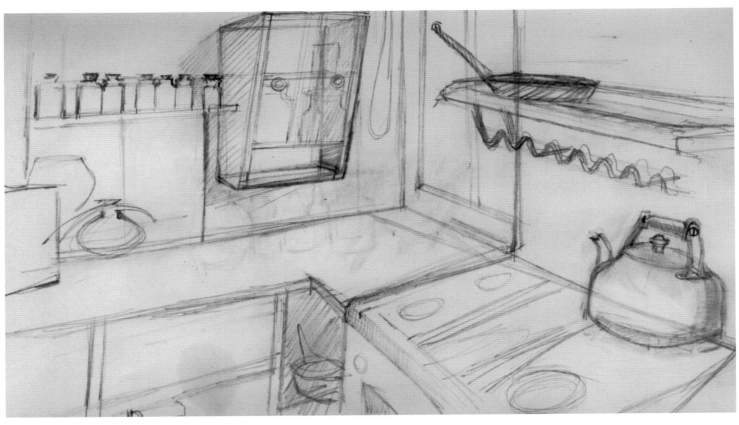

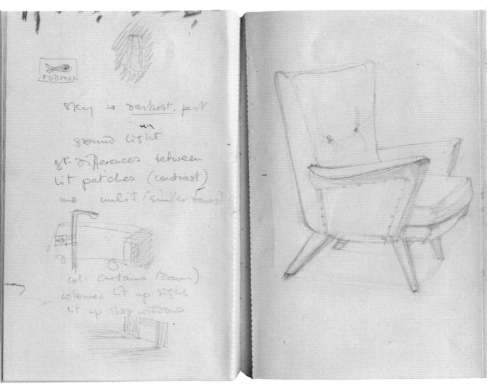

sky is darkest part

ground light

gt. differences between
lit patches (contrast)
and unlit (similar tones)

col. curtains (drawn)
coloured lit up signs
lit up shop windows

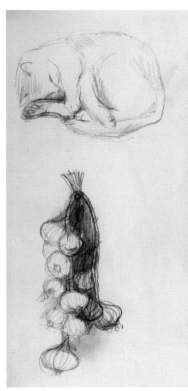

Drawings of our kitchen were the source material for the illustrations in Tiger

I did not really have great hopes for it. At the time I was more excited by a suggestion that I should audition for the voice-over on a German soap commercial, thinking of all the Christmas presents I would be able to buy with the money. However, the producer dismissed me out of hand, claiming that I spoke with a Liechtenstein accent (and I had never even been to Liechtenstein!) and I went home very cross – to find a message that Collins wanted to meet me to talk about the book.

Collins then had their offices in St James's Place. They consisted of two rather rickety houses joined together at the ground floor. Only the stairs were still separate, so if you went up the wrong flight, you had to come all the way down again before climbing up the other flight. At the top of the house Billy and Lady Collins had a flat where they could spend the night and sometimes entertained people to lunch.

I met the children's book editors Susan Dickinson and Julia MacRae. They said they liked the book, but had certain reservations. The general layout was wrong – the pictures were all squashed together – and in some of the illustrations the father looked totally unlike himself. And that business about the tiger drinking all the water in the tap... "Rather unrealistic," they said, which was odd in view of the rest of the story. Also they didn't like the title. I had called it *Tacy and the Tiger,* and they thought Tacy was too odd a name.

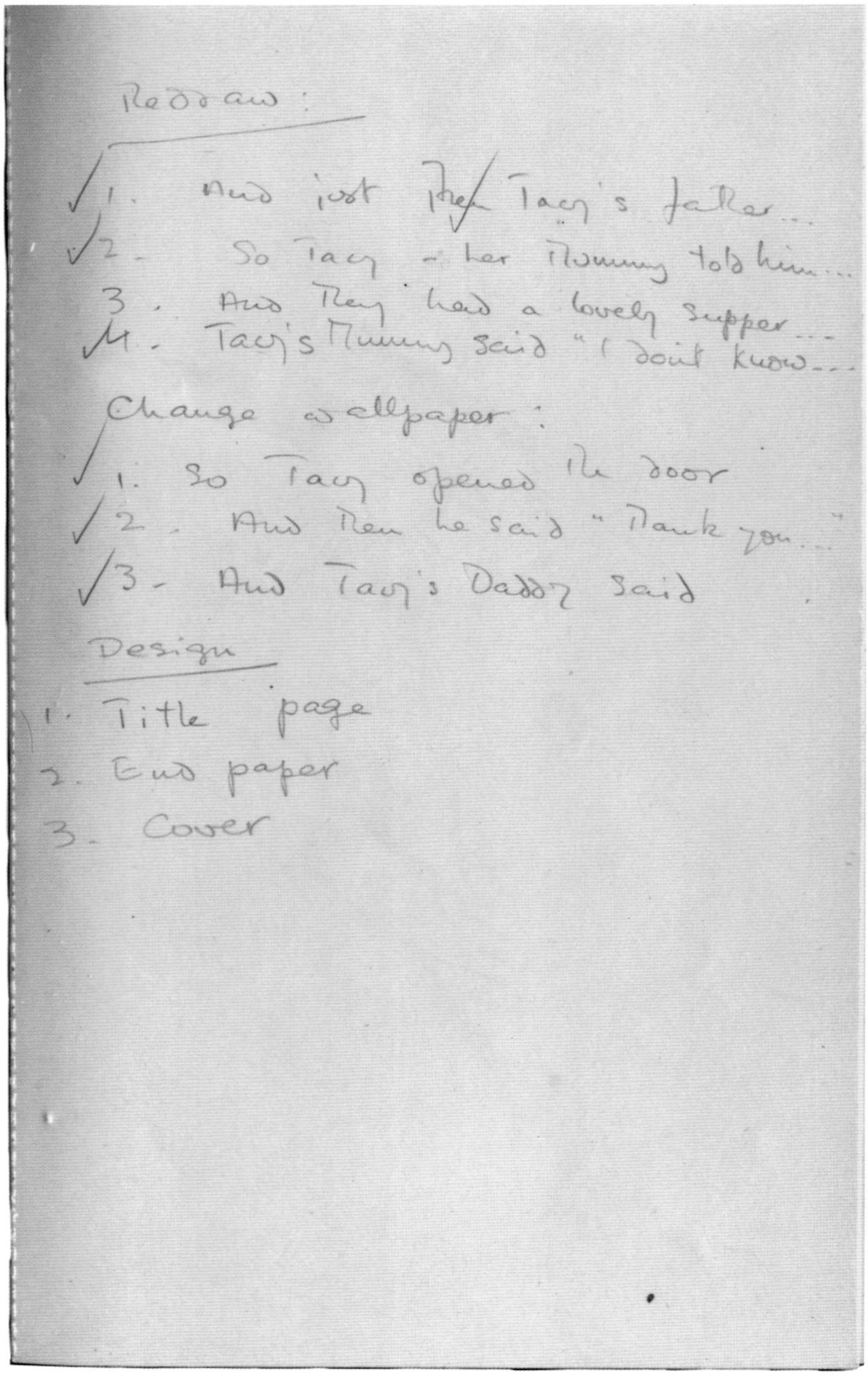

'To do' list after interview with Collins

Redraw:

✓1.   And just then Tacy's father...
✓2.   So Tacy – her Mummy told him...
 3.   And they had a lovely supper...
✓4.   Tacy's Mummy said "I don't know...

Change wallpaper:

✓1.   So Tacy opened the door
✓2.   And then he said "Thank you..."
✓3.   And Tacy's Daddy said

Design

1.   Title page
2.   End paper
3.   Cover

I said the bit about the water in the tap was the part my children liked best, and quickly tried to think of a name that scanned in the same way as Tacy. Finally I came up with Sophie. It turned out that Susan Dickinson had a daughter called Sophie, and I felt the reservations melt a little. And since *Sophie and the Tiger* didn't have quite the same ring as *Tacy and the Tiger*, we decided to call it simply *The Tiger Who Came to Tea*.

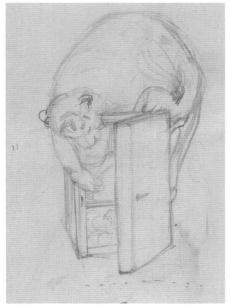

Above and left:
more drawings for Tiger

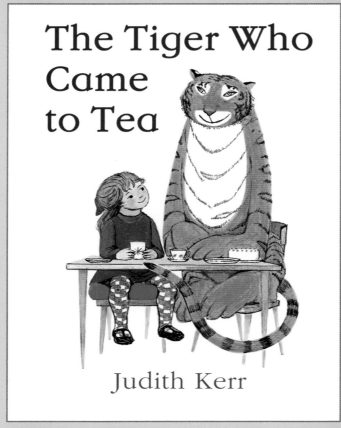

The Tiger Who Came to Tea

Judith Kerr

Cover

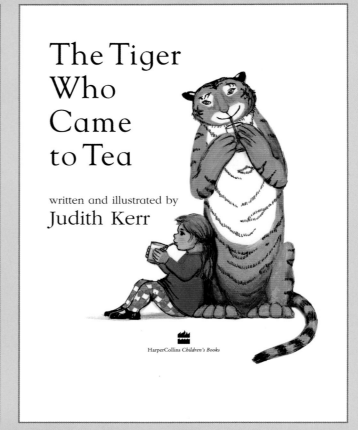

The Tiger Who Came to Tea

written and illustrated by
Judith Kerr

HarperCollins *Children's Books*

Page 3

For Tacy and Matty

Other books by Judith Kerr include:

Mog's Christmas	Mog and the V.E.T.
Mog and the Baby	Mog's Bad Thing
Mog in the Dark	Goodbye Mog
Mog's Amazing Birthday Caper	Birdie Halleluyah!
Mog and Bunny	Mog the Forgetful Cat
Mog and Barnaby	The Other Goose
Mog on Fox Night	Goose in a hole
Mog and the Granny	How Mrs Monkey Missed the Ark

First published in hardback in Great Britain by William Collins Sons & Co Ltd in 1968. First published in paperback by Picture Lions in 1973. This edition published in paperback by HarperCollins Children's Books in 2006.

7 9 10 8 6
ISBN-13: 978-000-721599-7
ISBN-10: 0-00-721599-1

Picture Lions is an imprint of the Children's Division, part of HarperCollins Publishers Ltd. HarperCollins Children's Books is a division of HarperCollins Publishers Ltd. Text and illustrations copyright © Kerr-Kneale Productions Ltd 1968.
The author/illustrator asserts the moral right to be identified as the author/illustrator of the work. A CIP catalogue record for this title is available from the British Library. All rights reserved. No part of this publication may be reproduced, stored in a retrieval system or transmitted in any form or by any means, electronic, mechanical, photocopying, recording or otherwise, without the prior permission of HarperCollins Publishers Ltd, 77-85 Fulham Palace Road, Hammersmith, London W6 8JB.

Visit our website at: www.harpercollinschildrensbooks.co.uk

Printed and bound in Singapore

Once there was a little girl called Sophie,
and she was having tea with her mummy
in the kitchen.
Suddenly there was a ring at the door.

Pages 4-5

Sophie's mummy said,
"I wonder who that can be.

And it can't be the boy from the grocer
because this isn't the day he comes.

It can't be the milkman
because he came this morning.

And it can't be Daddy
because he's got his key.

We'd better open the door and see."

Pages 6-7

Sophie opened the door, and there was a big, furry, stripy tiger. The tiger said, "Excuse me, but I'm very hungry. Do you think I could have tea with you?" Sophie's mummy said, "Of course, come in."

So the tiger came into the kitchen and sat down at the table.

Pages 8-9

Sophie's mummy said, "Would you like a sandwich?"
But the tiger didn't just take one sandwich.
He took all the sandwiches on the plate
and swallowed them in one big mouthful.
Owp!

And he still looked hungry,
so Sophie passed him the buns.

But again the tiger didn't eat just one bun.
He ate all the buns on the dish.
And then he ate all the biscuits
and all the cake,
until there was nothing
left to eat on the table.

So Sophie's mummy said,
"Would you like a drink?"
And the tiger drank
all the milk in the milk jug
and all the tea in the teapot.

And then he looked round the kitchen   to see what else he could find.

He ate all the supper
that was cooking in the saucepans…

…and all the food in the fridge,

…and all the packets and tins in the cupboard…

…and he drank all the milk,
and all the orange juice,
and all Daddy's beer,
and all the water in the tap.

Then he said,
"Thank you for my
nice tea. I think I'd
better go now."

And he went.

Sophie's mummy said, "I don't know what to do.
I've got nothing for Daddy's supper, the tiger has
eaten it all."

Pages 22-23

And Sophie found she couldn't have her bath
because the tiger had drunk all the water in the tap.

Just then Sophie's daddy came home.

Pages 24-25

So Sophie and her mummy told him what had happened, and how the tiger had eaten all the food and drunk all the drink.

And Sophie's daddy said, "I know what we'll do. I've got a very good idea. We'll put on our coats and go to a café."

Pages 26-27

So they went out in the dark, and all the street lamps were lit, and all the cars had their lights on, and they walked down the road to a café.

Pages 28-29

And they had a lovely supper with sausages and chips and ice cream.

In the morning Sophie and her mummy went shopping and they bought lots more things to eat.

And they also bought a very big tin of Tiger Food, in case the tiger should come to tea again.

GOOD-BYE...GOOD-BYE...GOOD-BYE...GOOD-BYE...

But he never did.

In the end we agreed that I would redraw the father where necessary and that there would also have to be two title pages and of course a cover design. I can't remember whether it was on this occasion or later that I talked about the book with Patsy Cohen, the art director, but whenever it was, I owe her a very great deal. With the greatest kindness and tact, she guided me through many of the facts and techniques of illustration that I had missed by never going to classes, and it was very much thanks to her that the book came out looking as good as it did.

Redrawing the father turned out to be a problem. I thought it would help if I could draw him from life, but Tom didn't have time to sit for me, so in the end I asked an actor friend, Alfie Burke, whether he would do it, and this worked well. However, if you look closely at the book, you can still clearly see which of the fathers are based on Tom and which on Alfie.

After various delays, *The Tiger Who Came to Tea* was published in October 1968. I had been warned by friends who knew about these things not to expect any reviews, so, when I looked through the Sunday papers on the relevant day and found none, I was not disappointed. However, it turned out that I had looked in the wrong part, and they rushed round to show us an enthusiastic one by Antonia Fraser, and we all had a celebratory lunch together.

I immediately started work on another book. It was about an imaginative small boy like Matthew who had bad dreams and nightmares, and it was called *The Crocodile Under the Bed*. It had nice drawings, but the story was very boring. Collins took it without much enthusiasm, but spent so much time considering that, by the time they had to make a final decision, I had produced a third book. (I was a lot faster then than I am now.) This one was more interesting, and they decided, wisely, to ditch *The Crocodile Under the Bed* and publish the new one instead. It was called *Mog the Forgetful Cat*.

Title page from the unpublished
The Crocodile Under the Bed

It was based – well, more or less based – on fact. I had always wanted a cat as a child, and Tom also loved cats, so, soon after moving into our house, we had acquired a rather eccentric cat called Mog. She almost never meowed, but made wonderfully expressive faces instead. She used her cat flap to get out, but utterly refused to use it on the way back in. And if she wanted her supper and we were watching television, she would simply hang her tail down in front of the screen. She also had a passion for boiled eggs. I thought it would be fun to do a book just about all the things she did. Only, I said to Tom, something would have to happen in the end. Tom was in the middle of work and just muttered, "Oh, let her catch a burglar." So, of course, I did.

Mog liked to sit on my lap while I worked.

Writing the story was very different from the *Tiger*, which had gradually evolved as a bedtime story. By this time both children had learned to read and, having myself learned to read in German, which is more or less phonetic, I had been very much struck by how much more difficult it is to learn to read in English. Matthew, stuck with *Janet and John*, one day had earnestly informed me, "I am sorry, Mummy, but I cannot read these books any more. They are too boring," and as I opened my mouth to say, "But you have to learn to read," had said, "I am going to learn to read with the *Cat in the Hat* books." (As he did.)

The Cat in the Hat by the incomparable Dr Seuss had been published in England by Billy Collins, to the disapproval at first of the *Janet and John* brigade of learning to read, who thought his almost cartoonish illustrations and wild rhyming stories a bit common. He used a limited vocabulary of simple words in wonderfully inventive ways, and he was *funny*. For the first time the huge effort of learning to read had been made worthwhile.

Above: Mog with boiled egg

I determined that, like Dr Seuss, I would use a vocabulary of no more than 250 words in the book about Mog, and I have done this with all my picture books since, with the exception of *Mog in the Dark* which, in a vain attempt to emulate *Green Eggs and Ham*, has a vocabulary of only just over fifty. I also determined never, ever to put anything in the text that the child could already tell from the pictures. Why should they struggle to read something they already knew?

With the knowledge I had gained from Patsy Cohen, I planned the book properly with a storyboard. I did a colour sketch of Mog's family, with the children based on Tacy and Matthew, though, after the problems with drawing Tom in *The Tiger Who Came to Tea*, it seemed wiser to base the parents on other people. I did a lot of sketches of Mog and of our house and its furnishings, and then I got on with the illustrations. *Mog the Forgetful Cat* was published in 1970, to good reviews.

Pages 87-91: the very first rough versions of Mog the Forgetful Cat

MOG

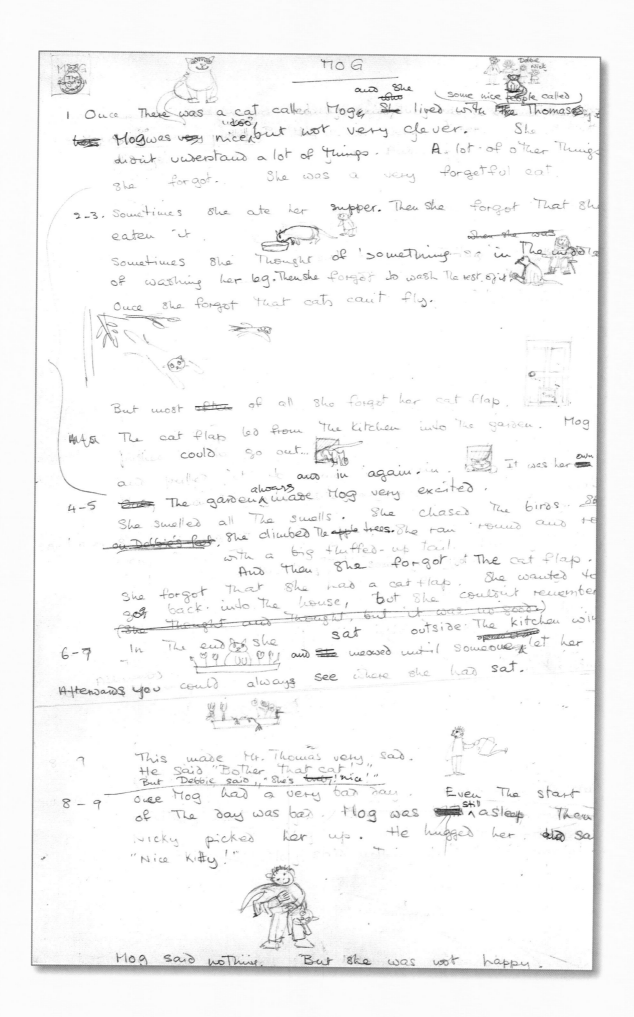

1 Once There was a cat called Mog. ~~She~~ and she lived with ~~the~~ Thomases (some nice ~~people~~ called)
~~Mog was very~~ Mog was ~~very~~ nice, but not very clever. She didn't understand a lot of things. A lot of other things she forgot. She was a very forgetful cat.

2-3. Sometimes she ate her supper. Then she forgot That she eaten it.
Sometimes she Thought of 'something ~~then she was~~ in The middle of washing her leg. Then she forgot to wash The rest of it.
Once she forgot that cats can't fly.

But most ~~of~~ of all she forgot her cat flap.
The cat flap led ~~from~~ The kitchen into the garden. Mog could go out... and ~~pull~~ and in again. ~~in.~~ It was her own
~~The~~ The garden always made Mog very excited.

4-5 She smelled all The smells. She chased The birds. ~~She~~ ~~on Debbie's~~ she climbed The ~~apple trees.~~ She ran round and ~~to~~ with a big fluffed-up tail.
And then she forgot The cat flap.
She forgot that she had a cat flap. She wanted to ~~got~~ back into The house, but she couldn't remember
~~She thought and thought, but it was no good.~~

6-7 In The end she sat outside The kitchen win~~dow~~ ~~and~~ meowed until someone let her
Afterwards you could always see where she had sat.

8 ? This made Mr. Thomas very sad.
He said "Bother that cat!"
But Debbie said, "She's ~~too~~ nice!"

8-9 Once Mog had a very bad day. Even The start of The day was bad. Mog was ~~still~~ asleep. Then Nicky picked her up. He hugged her. ~~and~~ sa~~id~~ "Nice Kitty!"

Mog said nothing. But she was not happy.

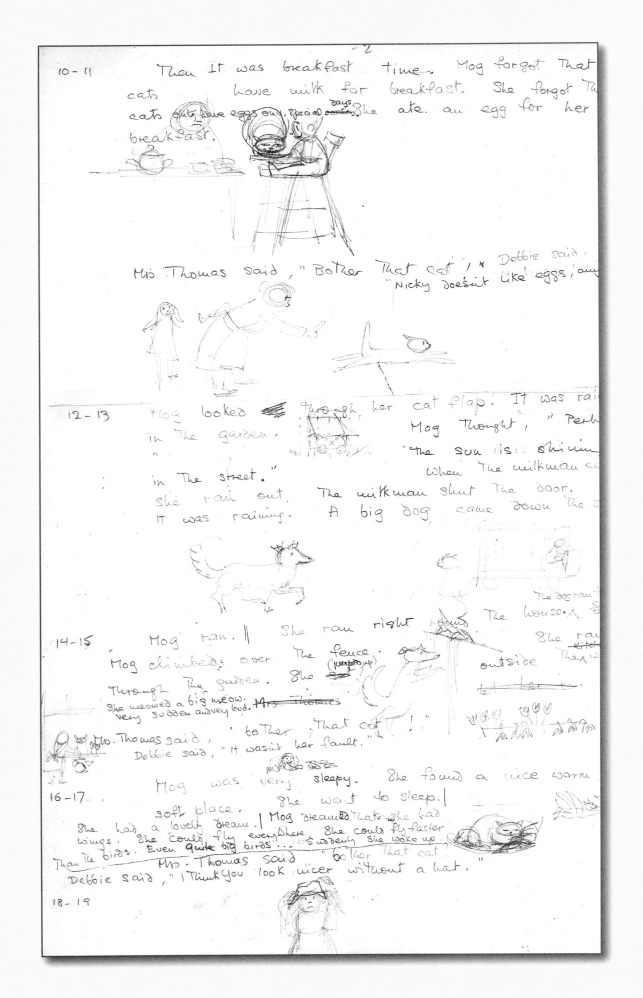

10-11 Then it was breakfast time. Mog forgot That
cats   have milk for breakfast. She forgot The
cats ~~only have eggs on~~ special days. She ate an egg for her
breakfast.

Mrs. Thomas said, "Bother That cat!" Debbie said,
"Nicky doesn't like eggs, any

12-13   Mog looked ~~through~~ her cat flap. It was rai
in The garden.   Mog Thought, "Perh
                      "The sun is shining
in The street."   When The milkman c
She ran out. The milkman shut The door.
It was raining.   A big dog came down The s

                                    The dog ran
                        She ran right ~~~~ The house.
14-15   Mog ran. | She ra
Mog climbed; over The fence. (jumps up)   outside Then
through The garden. She   ~~to her~~
She meowed a big meow. ~~Mrs. Thomas~~
very sudden and very loud.
Mrs. Thomas said,   "bother That cat !"
          Debbie said, "It wasn't her fault."

          Mog was very sleepy.   She found a nice warm
16-17.   soft place.   She went to sleep. |
She had a lovely dream. | Mog dreamed That she had
wings. She could fly everywhere she could fly faster
~~Than The birds. Even quite big birds...~~ Suddenly she woke up.
          Mrs. Thomas said, "bother That cat!"
Debbie said, "I Think you look nicer without a hat."

18-19

20-21 Nicky picked Mog up. He hugged her. He said "Nice kitty!" Mog said nothing. But she was not happy.

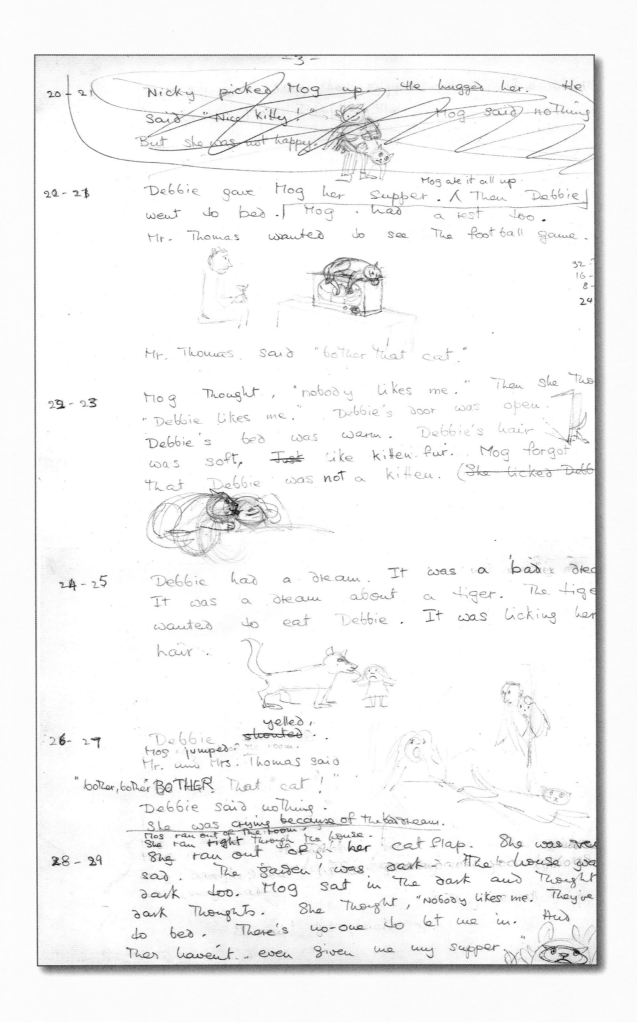

22-23 Debbie gave Mog her supper. Mog ate it all up. Then Debbie went to bed. Mog had a rest too.

Mr. Thomas wanted to see the football game.

Mr. Thomas said "bother that cat."

32-
16-
8-
24

22-23 Mog thought, "nobody likes me." Then she thought "Debbie likes me." Debbie's door was open. Debbie's bed was warm. Debbie's hair was soft, just like kitten fur. Mog forgot that Debbie was not a kitten. (She licked Debb

24-25 Debbie had a dream. It was a bad drea It was a dream about a tiger. The tige wanted to eat Debbie. It was licking her hair.

26-27 Debbie yelled shouted.
Mog jumped to room.
Mr. and Mrs. Thomas said
"bother, bother BOTHER that cat!"
Debbie said nothing.
She was crying because of the dream.

28-29 Mog ran out of the room.
She ran right through the house.
She ran out of her cat flap. She was ve sad. The garden was dark. The house wa dark too. Mog sat in the dark and thought dark thoughts. She thought, "Nobody likes me. They've to bed. There's no-one to let me in. And they haven't even given me my supper."

30-31   Then she noticed something. The house was v quik dark. There was a little light. It w moving about in the kitchen. She looked through the window. There was a man in the kitchen. He had a bag. He was putting ~~spoons into the bag~~. Mog thought, "perha that man will let me in. Perhaps he will give me my supper." ‖ She meowed her biggest meow. Very sudden and very, very loud.

The man was surprised. He dropped the bag
32-33   All sorts of ~~things~~ fell out. They made a big n
Everyone in the house woke up. Mr. Thomas said "It's a
The burglar said, "~~All right, Sir, I'll come quietly.~~" Mrs. Thomas telephoned the
"That cat". It upset me." police. Debbie let Mog in. Nicky hugge

34-35   A policeman came. ~~They told him what~~ ~~had happe~~ The policeman looked at Mog. He said.
"What a remarkable cat. I've seen watch-d but never a watch-cat. She will get a m

"I think she'd rather have a boiled egg," ~~said~~ Debbie Said
Mog had a medal. She also
had an ~~boiled~~ egg every day for break

36   Mr. and Mrs. Thomas told all their friends
about her. They said, "Mog is really remarkable." And T
never — (or almost never) — said, "Bother Tha

$11\frac{3}{4} \times 22\frac{3}{8}$ $\frac{£11}{1-2}$
                                         $\frac{}{8}$
                                      $\overline{12-11}$

Above: experiments with inks
and characters for Mog's family
with, below, a sketch of the children

Pages 92-95: storyboard for Mog the Forgetful Cat

falling leaves?

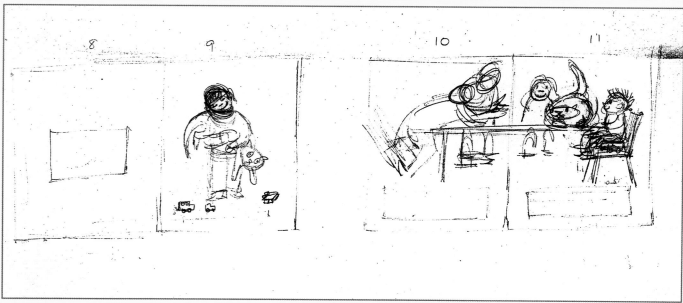

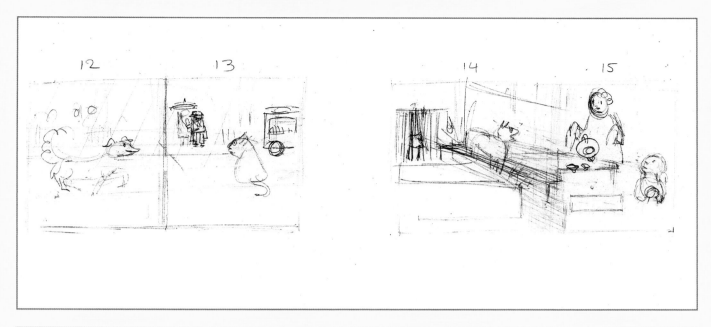

feathers on
wings =
feathers
on hat?

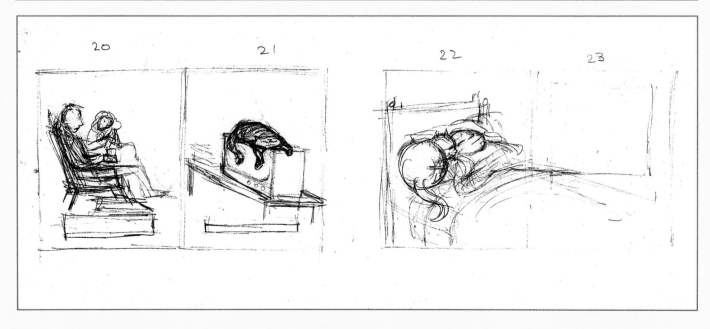

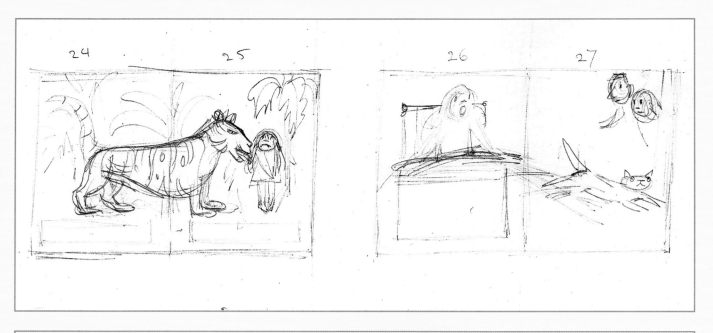

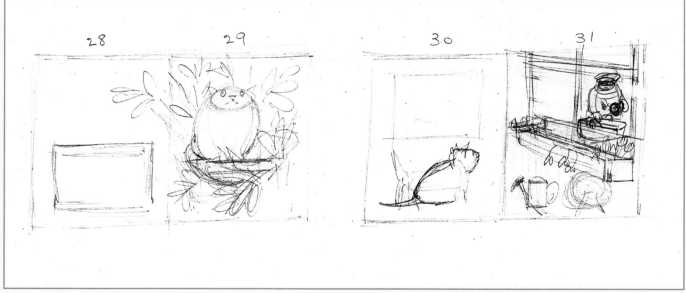

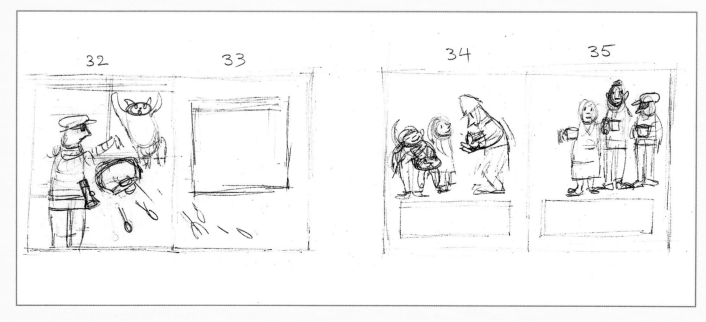

Early drawings of Mog

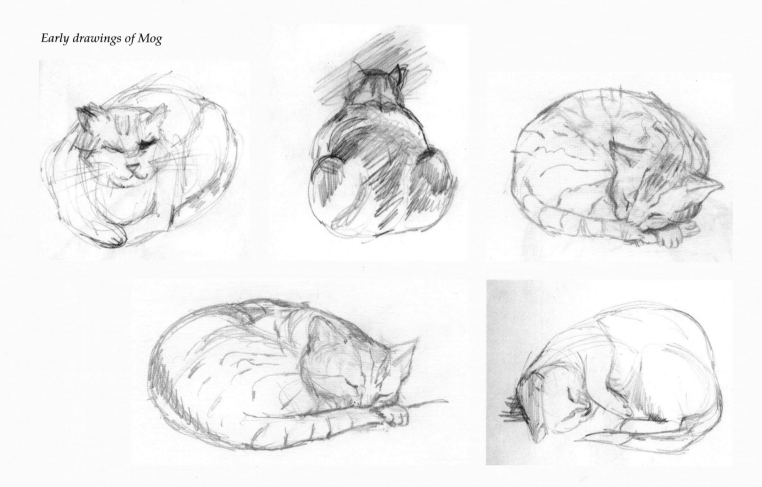

MOG
the Forgetful Cat

written and
illustrated by

Judith Kerr

HarperCollins *Children's Books*

Pages 2-3

For our own Mog

Other books by Judith Kerr include:

Mog's Christmas*

Mog and the Baby*

Mog in the Dark

Mog's Amazing Birthday Caper*

Mog and Bunny

Mog and Barnaby

Mog on Fox Night

Mog and the Granny

Mog and the V.E.T.*

Mog's Bad Thing*

Goodbye Mog

Birdie Halleluyah!

The Tiger Who Came to Tea*

The Other Goose

Goose in a Hole

Twinkles, Arthur and Puss*

One Night in the Zoo

*also available on audio CD.

First published in hardback in Great Britain by William Collins Sons & Co Ltd in 1970. First published in paperback in 1975 and in a new edition in 1993 by Picture Lions. Reissued by HarperCollins Children's Books in 2005. This edition published in 2010.

10 9 8 7 6 5 4 3 2

ISBN-13: 978-0-00-723721-0

Visit our website at: www.harpercollins.co.uk

Printed in China

Mr Thomas

Mrs Thomas

Nicky

Debbie

Once there was a cat called Mog.
She lived with a family called Thomas.
Mog was nice but not very clever.
She didn't understand a lot of things.
A lot of other things she forgot.
She was a very forgetful cat.

Pages 4-5

Sometimes she ate her supper.
Then she forgot that she had
eaten it.

Sometimes she thought of something
in the middle of washing her leg.
Then she forgot to wash the rest of it.

Once she forgot
that cats can't fly.

But most of all she forgot her cat flap.
The cat flap led from the kitchen
into the garden.
Mog could go out…

…and in
again.
It was
her
own
little
door.

The garden always made Mog very excited.
She smelled all the smells.
She chased the birds.
She climbed the trees.
She ran round and round
with a big fluffed-up tail.
And then she forgot the cat flap.
She forgot that she had a cat flap.
She wanted to go back into the house,
but she couldn't remember how.

Afterwards you could always tell
where she had sat.
This made Mr Thomas very sad.
He said, "Bother that cat!"
But Debbie said, "She's nice!"

In the end she sat outside the kitchen window
and meowed until someone let her in.

Once Mog had a very bad day.
Even the start of the day was bad.
Mog was still asleep.
Then Nicky picked her up.
He hugged her
and said, "Nice kitty!"
Mog said nothing.
But she was not happy.

Then it was breakfast time.
Mog forgot that cats have milk for breakfast.
She forgot that cats only have eggs as a treat.

She ate an egg for her breakfast.
Mrs Thomas said, "Bother that cat!"
Debbie said, "Nicky doesn't like eggs anyway."

Pages 14-15

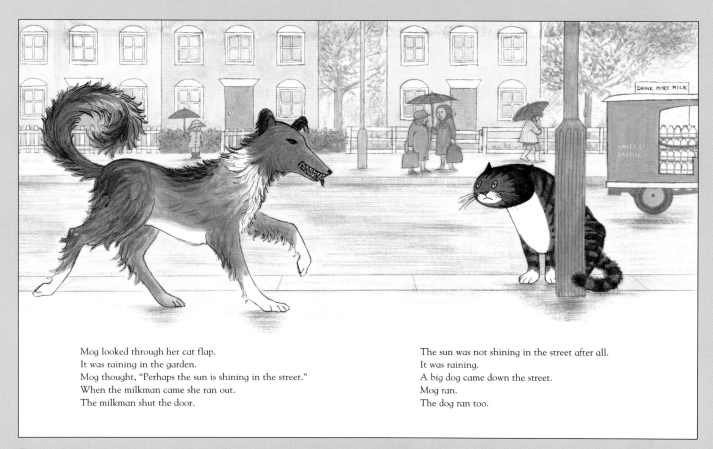

Mog looked through her cat flap.
It was raining in the garden.
Mog thought, "Perhaps the sun is shining in the street."
When the milkman came she ran out.
The milkman shut the door.

The sun was not shining in the street after all.
It was raining.
A big dog came down the street.
Mog ran.
The dog ran too.

Pages 16-17

Mog ran right round the house.
And the dog ran after her.
She climbed over the fence.
She ran through the garden
and jumped up outside the kitchen window.
She meowed a big meow,
very sudden and very loud.

Mrs Thomas said, "Bother that cat!"
Debbie said, "It wasn't her fault."

Pages 18-19

Mog was very sleepy.
She found a nice warm, soft place
and went to sleep.
She had a lovely dream.
Mog dreamed that she had wings.

She could fly everywhere.
She could fly faster than the birds,
even quite big birds…
Suddenly she woke up.

Pages 20-21

Mrs Thomas said, "Bother that cat!"
Debbie said, "I think you look nicer without a hat."

Debbie gave Mog her supper
and Mog ate it all up.
Then Debbie and Nicky went to bed.

Mog had a rest too,
but Mr Thomas wanted to see the fight.
Mr Thomas said, "Bother that cat!"

Mog thought, "Nobody likes me."
Then she thought, "Debbie likes me."
Debbie's door was open.

Debbie's bed was warm.
Debbie's hair was soft, like kitten fur.
Mog forgot that Debbie was not a kitten.

Pages 26-27

Debbie had a dream.
It was a bad dream.
It was a dream about a tiger.

The tiger wanted
to eat Debbie.
It was licking her hair.

Pages 28-29

Debbie shouted.
Mog jumped.
Mr and Mrs Thomas said,
"Bother, bother,
BOTHER that cat!"
Debbie said nothing.
She was still crying
because of the bad dream.

Pages 30-31

Mog ran out of the room
and right through the house
and out of her cat flap.
She was very sad.
The garden was dark.
The house was dark too.
Mog sat in the dark
and thought dark thoughts.
She thought, "Nobody likes me.
They've all gone to bed.
There's no one to let me in.
And they haven't even given me my supper."

Pages 32-33

Then she noticed something.
The house was not quite dark.
There was a little light moving about.
She looked through the window
and saw a man in the kitchen.
Mog thought, "Perhaps that man will let me in.
Perhaps he will give me my supper."

Pages 34-35

She meowed her biggest meow,
very sudden and very, very loud.
The man was surprised.
He dropped his bag.
It made a big noise
and everyone in the house woke up.

Mr Thomas ran down to the kitchen
and shouted, "A burglar!"
The burglar said, "Bother that cat!"
Mrs Thomas telephoned the police.
Debbie let Mog in
and Nicky hugged her.

Pages 36-37

A policeman came and they told him what had happened.
The policeman looked at Mog.
He said, "What a remarkable cat.

I've seen watch-dogs, but never a watch-cat.
She will get a medal."
Debbie said, "I think she'd rather have an egg."

Mog had a medal.
She also had an egg every day for breakfast.
Mr and Mrs Thomas told all their friends about her.
They said, "Mog is really remarkable."
And they never – (or almost never) – said, "Bother that cat!"

When Tacy and Matthew were twelve and nine, and well past the age of picture books, I had occasionally tried to tell them about my own childhood. Matthew thought it sounded rather interesting, but Tacy, who was very home-loving, thought it sounded dreadful and I could not explain to her that, in spite of some difficulties, I would not have missed it for the world. I began to think of writing a book about it, but it was a bit daunting, and I went to talk to Roger Benedictus who was then my editor, hoping for some sort of useful advice. However, all he said was, "Jolly good idea, we haven't got anything about that period," which was encouraging, but didn't really help.

I think it was about this time that we all went to see *The Sound of Music*. Tom and I watched it with a fair degree of horror, but Matthew, who was already very interested in history, came out looking very pleased and said, "Now we know exactly what it was like when Mummy was a little girl." This certainly seemed to make the writing of the book more urgent, but I still couldn't think how.

Then the children caught chicken pox and Tacy became quite ill with it, so that I spent a week or so sleeping in her room. It was full of her books, and while I knew vaguely what she was reading, I had only read some of them myself. While she was dozing, I picked up one she had talked about enthusiastically. It was *Little House on the Prairie* by Laura Ingalls Wilder, and I knew at once – this was it. This was the sort of book I wanted to write. A novel, written in the third person rather than the first, which gave one the freedom to leave out some minor happenings, while dramatising others, but which in all essentials would be totally truthful.

As always, it was difficult. Such ideas as I have tend to come to me in the afternoon, which was of course when the children came home from school, and in those days before freezers and takeaways and local supermarkets, I would find that I'd forgotten to shop and that yet again there was nothing for supper but cold ham. The first three chapters took me three months and the whole thing was such a strain that I said to Tom, "This isn't going to work." However, he read it (it was written in pencil, endlessly crossed out and in one or two places I had actually gone through the paper) and said, very unselfishly in view of the awful suppers, "No, it's good, you must finish it."

(Anna's official childhood?)

Anna's emigration.

1. Anna, coming home from school, with Midi.
Very happy - they had a good morning.
February 1933. Slushy snow. (The trams
have been on strike, but now they're working
again.) They stop at Frau Stark's station. Grown-up
conversation — shops — "1931 was bad, 1932
worse, 1933 will be worst of all." Someone asks
after Anna's father. (He has flu.) Hopes he'll
write in the paper again soon. Anna buys some
crayons — special — Happy. gossipy walk along
home. (She is soft, short, Frau Stark lets her
have it anyway, gossips with home.

Lunch at Anna's house. Her brother M.
already home with Günther, from his class
(Günther's family can't feed him so he has
lunch with a different better-off class-mate each day)
Mama + Heimpi preoccupied. political talk,
some minor Nazi outrages — Berlin. Anna
is bored. tries to impress quoting Frau Stark's prophecy — but
no-one takes much notice. telephone
rings just as they're finishing lunch.
Much running up and down to Papa, still ill in
bed. Mama has left half her pudding
and does not come back to finish it,
stays talking to Papa instead.
When Anna tries to go into the
bedroom she shoos her away.
Anna goes to the nursery and draws with her
later. she shows Papa what she has done,

new crayons.
(an illustrated
poem about
a disaster)

First notes for When Hitler Stole Pink Rabbit

It was strange, every day in my workroom, thinking myself back to my childhood, when I was the youngest child in a family of four, and then coming out to another family of four, where I was Mum. Also, I had never really imagined, as a mother, what those times when we were refugees had been like for my parents. Suddenly I thought, how would I have managed if I had had to get my children across the frontier? Less well, I am sure. And I was embarrassed by the way my parents were so different from the parents in *Little House on the Prairie* and other "proper" children's books, where, when things got hard, the mother could always cook and make the children's clothes and the father would chop wood and make furniture. Was one allowed, in a story, to have parents who were, on the whole, pretty impractical? When at last I got to the end I thought, I've described it all as truthfully as I can, but who on earth is going to want to read it?

I waited anxiously to hear what Collins thought of it. Eventually someone rang me up.

A voice talked at length about various aspects of the book, how this or that was interesting, until I could stand it no longer and asked, rather loudly, "Does that mean that you're going to publish it?" "Oh yes," said the voice, a bit hurt. "Of course."

Tom thought of the title *When Hitler Stole Pink Rabbit*. Nowadays everyone thinks it's a terrific title but at the time nobody liked it. However, as they couldn't think of anything better we were able to keep it. It was decided that there should be a line illustration at the head of every chapter, but there was only a short time in which to produce them and the school holidays had just begun. Luckily Tom was between scripts, and the children had a wonderful time being taken out by him every day, while I sat at home, frantically drawing. Patsy Cohen advised on the cover and had the brilliant idea of putting a pink rabbit waving a swastika flag on the spine. It was the last of my books that we worked on together. She retired soon afterwards, and I missed her sadly.

Opposite: cover rough for **When Hitler Stole Pink Rabbit**

This page: the finished cover artwork with Patsy Cohen's idea for the spine

When Hitler Stole Pink Rabbit was published in the autumn of 1971. The reviews were fine, and Billy Collins rang me up to say how much he liked it. Everyone seemed to agree that I had written a good book and I was terribly pleased with myself. (The only thing is, if they had all said it was awful, I would have believed that too.) And there was something else as well. As the book sold and was translated into other languages it began to earn money for me, and I thought, "I am earning money from my parents' hard times." And of course that money would have been a godsend to them in the period I had described. But neither my mother nor my father lived to see me become an author. I often think about them and hope that they would have been pleased.

Cover drawing for the American edition of When Hitler Stole Pink Rabbit

6

More Books

ORIGINALLY I HAD NOT MEANT to write any more about the past after *When Hitler Stole Pink Rabbit*, which ended happily, with my parents successfully in charge of our fate. I did not want to write about what happened afterwards – how the difficulties became too much for them and they could no longer cope. But then I thought, after all, being a refugee is not all fun and jollity, and, even though it all ended happily for my brother and me, their lives were destroyed, and it seemed right that this, too, should be told. I always knew that if one wrote about it at all, there would have to be two books, one about my family in the war and one about what happened to them afterwards. Both would be hard to write, and I decided to alternate them with picture books.

I can't remember where the idea for *When Willy Went to the Wedding* came from, or indeed much about working on it, except that all my original drawings got lost during its production. As a result it was not republished until fairly recently, when the process of reproduction from printed images had become more sophisticated. *Bombs on Aunt Dainty* (originally called *The Other Way Round*, a title so unmemorable that even I could never remember it) was a much longer book than *Pink Rabbit* and took me well over a year to write.

On the day I finished it, I got a call from my German publishers that *Pink Rabbit* had won the German Youth Book Prize.

Pink Rabbit had not at first had any luck in Germany. When shown it at the Frankfurt Book Fair, my German publishers Ravensburger had taken one look and, possibly at the sight of Patsy Cohen's rabbit waving a swastika, had dropped the book in horror and refused even to read it. However, the following year they had a new editor. This was Hans-Christian Kirsch, himself a writer and winner of the Youth Book Prize. He was also the son of one of Hitler's generals and remembered how his father had to attend Hitler once every few weeks, and how his family wondered each time whether he would emerge from these meetings alive.

Hans-Christian immediately decided to publish the book, "with not a word altered," he said. (This was in contrast to a French translation, which had called the book *Three Countries for Little Anna* and removed all references to Hitler or the Nazis.) He commissioned a very good translation from Annemarie Böll, wife of the distinguished novelist Heinrich Böll, and the book came out in 1974. Unlike now, when the Holocaust is almost obsessively taught in German schools, people until then had shied away from talking to children about the Nazis, and the book was an easy introduction to what had largely been a taboo subject.

There was an award ceremony, and Tom and I went to it. I had been back to Germany a number of times since the war, nearly always on unhappy occasions. The first time was for my father's funeral in 1948. Then my brother and I, with the help of the British Control Commission, had travelled to Hamburg through the devastated Ruhr, and though nowadays it seems callous, at the time we had felt nothing but satisfaction at the total destruction of Hitler's Germany. At the ceremony I remember my father's coffin draped in the Union Jack, and thinking, "I really must write and tell him about that." Also my first meetings with Germans since the war, and wondering always what part they had played in the horrors of the past.

Portrait of my mother, 1947

The second time had been for my mother. She had remained in Germany after my father's death and had bravely made a new career for herself as an interpreter, first for the Americans and later for the new democratic government of West Berlin. However in 1956 she took an overdose of sleeping tablets, and I had rushed to Berlin and stayed with her until she recovered. Again I had met Germans, and again with the same suspiciousness.

After this, though my mother often came to visit us in England, I always avoided visiting her in Berlin, giving the needs of my family as an excuse, but really because I always felt uneasy there. However in 1965, a few days after she had returned to Berlin from a stay with

Wall decorations in the Judith Kerr School in Berlin using pictures from my ABC book

us in London, she collapsed with a heart attack in the middle of a game of tennis and died aged only sixty-seven. I went with my brother to the funeral, leaving Tom to look after the children. It was a bleak occasion, made only slightly better by our knowledge that, since she had a horror of growing old, she would probably have approved of the way things had happened. She had made good German friends over the years, some of them distinguished admirers of my father, all of whom came to her funeral, and it was clear that Germany – at least West Berlin – had become a very different place. But when I left to come home to London I could see no reason ever to return.

The Youth Book Prize changed all this. Not only did it feel quite different going to Germany for such a happy reason, but by 1974 a new generation had grown up which had not been involved in any Nazi horrors. I remember almost nothing about the award, but I vividly remember meeting these new Germans – admirable people deeply concerned about the events of what was by now a quite distant past. Because of the prize I was asked to speak in schools, and I met teachers and young people endlessly asking themselves how the Nazi horrors could have happened and how one could prevent them ever happening again in the future. I am still meeting them now, and find myself telling them that they really must stop feeling guilty about things that happened before even their parents were born.

There have been two more links with Germany since the Youth Book Prize. In 1992 I got a letter from the headmistress of a newly founded primary school in Berlin. It seemed that the staff and children had been given a vote on what to call their new school and had come up with my name. There was only one snag, wrote the headmistress: there was a rule that in Berlin schools could only be named after people who were dead. When I told Tom, he said, "That's asking too much!" However, the rule was relaxed, and we went to the opening, and found not only a remarkable bilingual establishment (the children were taught in both French and German), but also walls covered with murals based on some of my illustrations. I can take no credit for it, but it appears that the school has gone from strength to strength and is now one of the most popular in Berlin.

The last link came as a result of my father's work. In 1996 his books were being gradually republished, and the man in charge was a very good writer on the theatre called Gunther Ruhle. He discovered, hidden away in some cellar, a mass of weekly articles which my father had written for the chief newspaper in his home town Breslau, after he had first arrived in Berlin. The articles were written in the 1890s when Berlin had only recently become the capital of Germany, and dealt partly with the theatre, but mainly with everyday happenings like the introduction of electric light in the streets, and the Kaiser (whom my father could not stand). They were wise and entertaining, and, almost exactly a hundred years later, Berlin was again going through the same process of becoming the capital of Germany, which gave them a strange echo. They had never been published in book form, and Gunther decided to do so. Unlike my father's other reprinted books, which had commanded admiration rather than large royalties, the book became a bestseller.

Suddenly there was a large and totally unexpected sum of money, and my brother and I both felt that it should stay in Germany and be used in some way to remember our father. Only we couldn't think how. It was Tom, who had never known my father, who came up with the answer, which was to create a prize for an outstanding young actor. As soon as he said it, we knew it was right. Various excellent people in Berlin helped to set it up, and now the prize is awarded every year in Berlin, and I often go over for it and make a speech in dubious German and meet the actors, nearly all of whom have had distinguished careers since.

Ravensburger also published *Bombs on Aunt Dainty* and the third novel, *A Small Person Far Away*. Hans-Christian Kirsch and my publisher Christian Stottele visited us in London and became our friends. It is a long time since I felt uneasy in Germany. It is a different country from the one I left as a child, and if ever I sense the old uncertainty, I have only to remind myself that, since most of the Nazis must have been older than me, now that I am nearly ninety, there really can't be many of them left.

After the excitement of the Youth Book Prize and finishing *Bombs on Aunt Dainty*, I began work on a new picture book. It was inspired by our second cat, a muscular black and white called Wienitz. I think she was originally called Weenits because she was little, but then she grew and Tom insisted that she had aristocratic Viennese connections, and the spelling changed. All cats are weird, and Wienitz was weirder than most. For one thing, she was frightened of heights. She would start to climb up the apple tree in the garden and then look down in horror to see her bottom all of eight inches off the ground, and quickly slide and scramble back down. Once, for some reason she had got herself stuck on a first floor windowsill and Tom had to rescue her down a ladder, where she clung with all her paws to every rung and had to be disengaged with great difficulty.

She did not believe in hunting, but was partial to green beans, which she decided to regard as prey. When given one, she would deliberately turn her back to it and after a moment, having lulled the bean into false security, she would suddenly turn and pounce and devour it. (I never managed to get that into a book – it was too weird.) She did not like people outside the family and tended to observe

Above: Tacy and Matthew with Wienitz

Overleaf: an illustration from Mog's Christmas

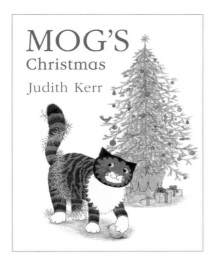

them for quite a long time and then bite them, but mainly she hated Christmas and was frightened of the Christmas tree.

I had never meant for Mog to be a series, but, rather than write a story about another cat and another family, it seemed simpler to attribute some of Wienitz's traits to Mog, and so I called the new book *Mog's Christmas*. Later various other cats also inspired stories. I am now on my ninth cat, so between all of them there has been plenty of material to draw on. A few of the Mog stories are largely invention, but the best ones are all fairly solidly based on something that actually happened.

Bombs on Aunt Dainty, which dealt with my teenage years, had been written when my children were teenagers. *A Small Person Far Away* is really a grown-up novel and I have always been pleased that my grown-up children liked it best of the three. All the books deal with the rise and fall of Hitler and its aftermath. But I never thought they should be about politics, or what is now history. I just wanted to tell the story of my family – how, when my brother and I were young, our parents were always able to protect us, how they always seemed to know what to do, and how, gradually the relationship changed, until, with my mother's attempt at suicide, the position was totally

reversed, and we became the grown-ups. Clearly something similar happens in all families, but if one has spent one's childhood as a refugee in a succession of strange countries, one's family feels like an island separate from the rest of the world, and I suppose that makes everything more intense.

A Small Person Far Away was published in 1978 and, compared with *Bombs on Aunt Dainty* which was again nominated for the German Youth Book Prize, had fewer readers, but I had found writing it interesting and decided to follow it up with another grown-up novel: nothing to do with my family this time, but pure fiction.

This turned out not to have been a good idea. I spent about eighteen months on that book. There was nothing wrong with it. It had a perfectly good plot and some reasonably interesting characters. It was the sort of book that I might have quite enjoyed reading. It was just that there did not seem to be any real need for me to write it. I had at first written it in the third person. Then I cut some bits and added others. Then I wrote a prologue. Then I rewrote it in the first person. Each time about halfway through, I ran out of steam. Finally I had to admit that this particular book had no wish to be written by me, and gave up.

Rough drawing for the cover of Bombs on Aunt Dainty

Fortunately I had something else to fall back on. For some years I had had a new editor, Linda Davis. We had become friends with her and her husband Christopher, who was later to run Dorling Kindersley. She had had a baby the previous year and one day brought Ben round for tea. He was enchanted by Wienitz and followed her everywhere. They ended up next to each other on the sofa, and, true to type, Wienitz, after some consideration, bit him. Not hard – very little blood was shed – but just enough to express an opinion. So I wrote *Mog and the Baby*, but I should explain that the baby's mother in the book is not remotely based on Linda.

My failed novel must have had a powerful effect on me, for I see that during the following eight years I produced nothing but Mog books – six of them. However, some of them were also ways of experimenting with different kinds of picture books. *Mog in the Dark* was an attempt to use no more than about fifty different words, and I have been delighted a few times, when children have told me that this was the book that taught them to read. But some children also found it frightening. My small niece was horrified by the idea of birds with teeth, and when I said, "But there aren't any, really," answered darkly, "Well, not in London."

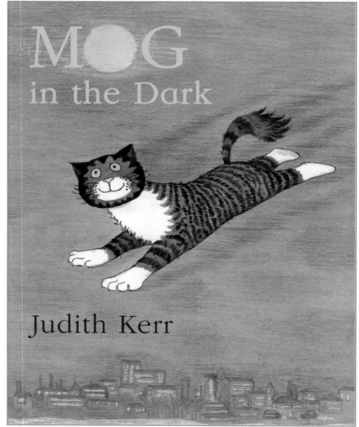

Birds with teeth

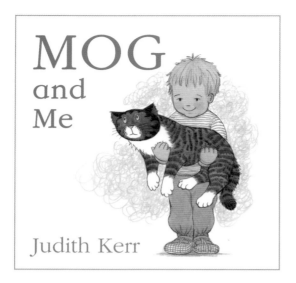

Then Linda wanted to introduce some small board books for very young children, and I produced *Mog and Me* and *Mog's Family of Cats*. It was quite interesting working to a different shape and trying to keep the contents down to what even a one-year-old could understand. *Mog's Amazing Birthday Caper* was an ABC book, made more complicated by the fact that, since by now Ravensburger were publishing my picture books, it needed to work also in German, and that was interesting too. *Mog and Barnaby* was a flap book, technically complicated to do – I finally had to buy a copier to make it work. Nowadays such books are of course manufactured by professionals, and it is the only Mog book out of print.

"He wants...

...to play!"

This page and following: roughs and finished
spreads from Mog and Barnaby

"He won't hurt you!

He likes you!"

"He won't hurt you!

He likes you!"

124

125

In the meantime, Tom was producing some of his most distinguished work – *The Road*, in which some eighteenth-century scientists are haunted by the vision of nuclear destruction in the future; *The Year of the Sex Olympics*, which in 1968 foretold reality television; *Wine of India*, in which medicine has advanced to a point where people can be kept in perfect health more or less permanently, but have their lives rationed according to how useful they are. (The present has almost caught up with that one.) And finally *The Stone Tape*, a very dark modern ghost story.

Still from The Road, *1963*

He also wrote a film script of *Tai-Pan* for Carlo Ponti, and was paid so much in expenses that the children and I were able to join him in Rome. Ponti had an American co-producer, but the two of them hated each other and kept having rows, so Tom had a lot of free time in which to show Rome to the children. Eight-year-old Matthew loved it all and said, "When I am grown up I am going to live here," and in fact this is what he has done. He has lived there with his family for more than ten years.

When the children were due to go back to school, we came home, leaving Tom in Rome with the producers still fighting. By now the argument was about a pirate raid in the script. One producer refused absolutely to make the film without the pirates. The other refused absolutely to leave them in. So Tom wrote two versions, one with pirates and one without, sent them both off to the relevant people and caught the next plane home. The film, not surprisingly, was never made, but we had all had a wonderful time.

Above: the brand new Bunny and,
right, slightly used with Posy

Below: Bunny having his bedtime milk

The children changed schools and grew up. Mog and Wienitz both died and we mourned them, but eventually got a new kitten called Posy. Posy was obsessed with having kittens. From quite an early age, she was giving the eye to various roving toms, and the vet, anxious that she might damage her health by having kittens before she was ready, gave her an injection to delay her development. Nothing daunted, she made do with Bunny. Bunny was a furry cat toy, which started out with feet and ears, but was soon reduced to a body and a head. Even so, Posy decided that it was a kitten. It came with her wherever she went. You could hear her coming as she talked to it – a sort of mrum mrum mrum noise – while carrying it in her mouth. It slept with her in her basket at night and she regularly dropped it in her milk bowl to feed it.

Mog liked Bunny.

She played with him...

She carried him about.

and played with him...

and played...

and played with him.

and played...

He was her best thing.

Finally one night she had her wish and produced five sons. We found them in the morning. She had laid them neatly out in a row, and at the end of the row was Bunny. Cats have an instinct to protect their young from predators by moving them to a higher level soon after their birth, and Bunny was the first to be carried to safety in this way. The kittens grew fat and bouncy as Posy fed them and washed them and kept them safe, but Posy became thinner and thinner, and we were advised by the vet to find homes for them as soon as possible, which we did. We just kept one called Felix. And, of course Bunny.

I think it was as Felix developed skills that Posy first noticed that Bunny was somewhat lacking in them. Felix was a demanding and affectionate son, and she must also have noticed that Bunny was less responsive. Anyway, one day Bunny disappeared. We looked for him for a while and then gave up. But a week later I found him in the garden. He had been carefully half-hidden in a far corner and next to him was a dead mouse. She must have decided that it was time he made his own way in the world, but had given him the best possible start.

After this it was not difficult to write *Mog and Bunny*. I used an earlier episode in his life when, on a wildly rainy night, Posy had appealed to me to come out into the garden, where she led me to a totally sodden Bunny. She evidently found him too wet to pick up, so I brought him inside and dried him on the radiator. He had been grey to start with, but became ever more mud-coloured with use, especially after his night in the rain. In the book, however, I made him pink, so as to show up against Mog's fur. But I never made a connection with *Pink Rabbit*.

7

Scripts and a Lot About Cats

WHAT CAN YOU SAY ABOUT a life that consists of two people sitting in adjoining rooms for forty-odd years, making marks on bits of paper? "Then he wrote this… and then I drew that…" Once we no longer had the children coming home from school to keep us in touch with the world, we often spent whole days speaking only to each other. Of course there were outings – to see Tacy act at drama school, to visit Matthew at Oxford, to see films and plays, and to see friends. But basically it was a pretty monastic existence.

We travelled, to New York, to LA, where Tom wrote *Halloween III* (but later took his name off, after various horrors including a head drilling scene were introduced). Later we went to Japan, where Matthew, while teaching English, was writing his first short stories. We saw Tacy act in the theatre and on television. And we had holidays in Portugal, in Greece, in Venice (but mostly in Venice). But we always came back to our two rooms and the next bit of work. Tom looked at my pictures and often had good, funny ideas, which I always used. I was less help to him, but I loved listening to the stories of plays he was planning to write, and became terribly frustrated if someone rang up while he was in the middle of one, because I wanted to know what happened next.

When we made audio tapes of my picture books, Tom did some of the voices. I remember he was particularly good as the burglar in *Mog the Forgetful Cat*. The stories were read by the

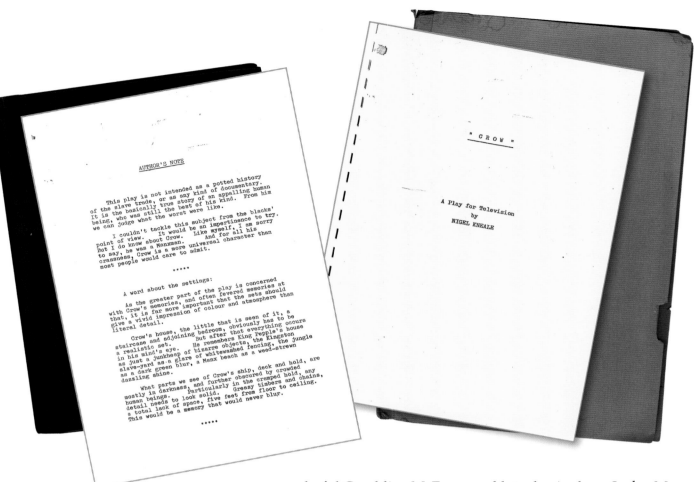

wonderful Geraldine McEwan and later by Andrew Sachs. My own job was limited to doing the meows.

Scriptwriting is a more dangerous occupation than producing picture books. The worst thing that can happen to you as an illustrator is that your work will be badly printed. The success of a script depends on so many things – the director, the actors, and most of all money. At one time Tom wrote a film script for *Brave New World*, to be directed by Jack Cardiff. It was to be shot in Spain. Everything was organised. Jack Cardiff was already out there. They had found us a flat in Madrid and even an English school for Tacy to go to. Then Jack Cardiff rang up and said, "They're selling the cars!" The company had gone bankrupt. We took the children on holiday to Southwold instead, but it was not the same.

Some years earlier Tom had been planning a film with Tony Richardson, when Ealing Films collapsed. After *Brave New World* he began to feel he was a bit of a jinx. And *Crow*, his very good television play about the slave trade, was cancelled days before rehearsals were due to start, because of a row between management and the designer. All this must have been terribly disheartening, but Tom just went on writing. Which was just as well, as the money I earned from my picture books went nowhere. Tom kept us all, and I could never have done the books if he hadn't supported me and the children all those years until they were grown up.

Below: rough from **Mrs Monkey** *and, above and right, finished pictures*

After the six Mog books, I finally thought I'd do something different and spent some time on a book called *How Mrs Monkey Missed The Ark*. I made Mrs Monkey a sort of yiddisher momma, who fussed so much about finding a little fruit for the journey that the ark

For Adelie with love from Quentin Ken

left without her. The original edition was never quite right, but it was later completely redesigned with a new cover and a pull-out flap and looked rather nice.

It turned out quite well in the end.

"Now you must call the animals," said God.
"There will be two of each kind."
So Noah called the animals, and they all came and stood and looked at each other and wondered what would happen next.
And just then it started to rain.
"See?" said God.

Above: rough for **Mog on Fox Night** *and, below, the artwork*

ox: lemon + orange + 065 + 059 + 050 + 0
bs: orange + orange + 059

ky: cobalt + carmine + cobalt
       + 159 + 120 + black

mow: cobalt + 159 + black

y cubs:
    Burnt Sienna + orange + 059

what would happen if
   no black pen outlines
              against background?
    or dk. grey?

Above: colour tests for Mog on Fox Night

Then Posy's son Felix struck up a friendship with a fox. We were woken by a noise one night, and when we looked out of the window saw Felix and a large fox sitting side by side under a lamp post. We were not sure if that was all right, so we went downstairs and peered out of the front door. Felix immediately came over to us and scolded us for interfering in his social life, while the fox strolled slowly to the other side of the road, so we withdrew but sneaked a look from behind the curtains. The fox had come back and they were sitting under the lamp post as before.

After this Felix demanded his supper impatiently every night, so that he could go out and keep his appointment with his friend. I don't know what Posy thought about it, but of course it was too good to waste, and I wrote *Mog on Fox Night*. We found a fox rescue centre in the country, where they let me draw the foxes, which was lovely. Up till then, all my picture books had been published in German by Ravensburger, but I think at this point there must have been a new editor, and she turned the book down. She wrote me a letter in not very good English in which she said, "Foxes do not go in people's houses."

It so happened that I had just read a newspaper article about a woman who regularly fed a fox. One evening she was watching television when she heard a noise at the back door and found the fox looking hungry, but by the time she had fetched him something to eat, he had disappeared. Thinking that he had got tired of waiting, she went back to the living room, to find the fox sitting in her armchair. She quickly got her camera and took a picture of him, and the paper published it together with her account. So I cut out the article and sent it to the German editor. But she never replied.

In 1992 I had a great stroke of luck, as Collins appointed the great Ian Craig as my art editor. It turned out that we thought alike on a great many things, which made working together a joy. We have now been working together for twenty years, during which he has struggled to fill the many remaining gaps in my education, due to my never having gone to illustration classes. He has designed all my books and usually thinks of what should go on the cover and he always knows the answer when I am stuck. He is now also my editor, and is an inspiration and a friend.

Right: pages from
Mog and the Granny.
Dan Snow was the model for the war-dancing Red Indians

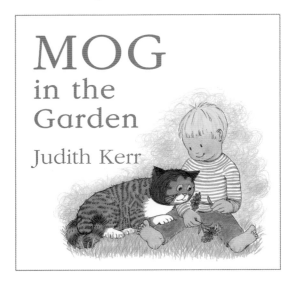

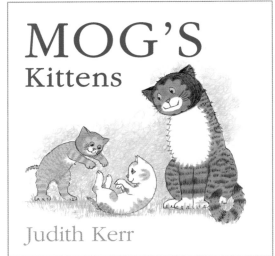

After *Fox Night* there was a demand from Collins for two more little board books, and I produced *Mog in the Garden* and *Mog's Kittens*. Tom and I were doing quite a number of trips at that time, and we noticed that no matter when we arrived home, Posy was always waiting for us by the gate. Mog in her time had done the same thing. It was as though they had some sort of second sight which told them when we were coming, and it seemed like a good idea for a book. Part of the idea had been that Mog's family should go to Disneyland, and Mog would be horrified by visions of a giant Mickey Mouse, which would have been quite funny. However, by the time I found out that Disney of course would never allow Mickey Mouse to be used in this way, the book had gone too far to stop, and I had to make do with a Red Indian display instead. Six-year-old Dan Snow (who now makes brilliant television programmes) posed for me in his Red Indian suit, but even so, the book never felt quite right. It was called *Mog and the Granny*.

Suddenly a picture of Debbie came into her head.
Debbie was smiling at a big bird.
Mog knew it was a bird because it had feathers.
But it had a face like a person. It was a person bird.
And there were more person birds nearby.
Why was Debbie smiling? Those big person birds
might fly away with her and hurt her.

The person birds had not hurt her at all.
Instead they had given her some of their feathers
and a baby person bird as a present. She was
smiling and excited, and she was coming home.
Mog thought, "I must be there to meet her."

She ran out of the yard

and across a road

and down another road

Roughs and finished pictures from Mog and the Granny

The next one, *Mog and the V. E. T.* was more solidly based. All our cats loathed being taken to the vet and always seemed to make more noise in the waiting room than any of the other animals, even though the vet was extremely nice. He allowed me to sketch his surgery and to sit in on some of his sessions with cats, which was a great help. Afterwards I gave him a copy of the book, but I am not sure how much he liked it. Perhaps it is unprofessional for a vet to let himself be bitten by one of his clients.

Illustration from Mog *and the V. E. T.* Note vet with bandaged finger

In spite, or perhaps because of, my irreligious upbringing, I have always been fascinated by angels, and loved drawing them even as a child. Apart from flying among the clouds, some small and quite tubby, and others huge and statuesque, one was never quite sure exactly what they did. Clearly some were more active than others, and so I thought it would be fun to do a book about a slightly absent-minded guardian angel.

At first the angel did not have a name, but then for some reason he had to have one, and I remembered a conversation I had once had with Matthew while driving the children home from school. I had asked, "What are you doing in English this term?" and he answered, "We're doing Birdie Halleluyah." "Birdie Halleluyah?" "Yes. Haven't you heard of Birdie Halleluyah? He lived in a cabin in the woods and wrote poetry and all sorts of stories." I had not heard of Birdie Halleluyah and asked if he was good, and Matthew said, yes, quite good, and then both children burst into wild giggles, because Birdie Halleluyah was pure invention, made up on the spur of the moment. Trying to think of a name for the angel, it suddenly occurred to me that Matthew's invention might be rather a good name for him, and so the book was called *Birdie Halleluyah*. Ian had suggested using gold on the angels, and it really looked rather good. I really liked that book, but it didn't do particularly well. Angels, apparently, don't sell.

Opposite and overleaf: successive stages in the creation of an elaborate composition for Birdie Halleluyah

Below: exhausted guardian angel (not used in the book)

140

Sunday 12.30pm

Monday 9.50am

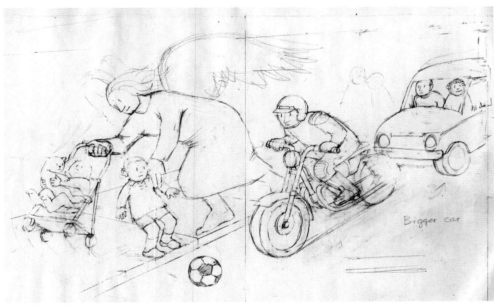

Monday 6.20pm

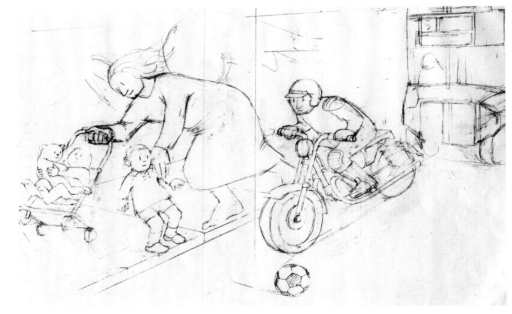

Tuesday 7.00pm

Wednesday 1.10pm

Thursday 7.40am

Thursday 11.30pm

Friday 7.00am

The finished piece

143

Finished artwork

Drawing for gold on wings

Printed book

The summer of 1995 was very hot. The hot weather went on and on, and Felix who, unlike his mother, was a great hunter, spent the nights roaming and bringing back prey. To our regret, he tended to go in for protected species and once proudly presented us with a dead woodpecker – the only one ever seen in our garden – and another time with a bat. But one night he must have roamed too far and tried to cross the main road. A car got him, and we found him dead next morning.

We were all distraught. He had been Tom's cat and used to sit on his lap with his paws on Tom's shoulders and gaze into his eyes. But it was worst for poor Posy. We showed her the body, but she did not recognise it as Felix, and just kept mewing and searching for him day after day. In the end we thought the only thing was to get her another kitten, and we found one that looked exactly like Felix. But this turned out to be a terrible mistake. They loathed each other on sight. Unlike Felix who had always had a certain gravitas, Leo the kitten was a silly little thing that rushed wildly about for no particular reason and had very little sense. Posy by now was becoming slightly elderly, and as Leo grew bigger and stronger, he bullied her, and she grew anxious and timid.

It all came to a head on Tom's birthday. We had never made much of birthdays before. I had tried to organise a party for him on his seventieth, but his agent Douglas Rae forbade it because Tom was still doing a lot of work, and he thought it would be a mistake to advertise his age to the film industry in which, he said, everyone was about twelve. So we had to wait for his seventy-fifth. As we had never done anything much before, we thought we'd go to town and hire a marquee.

The marquee was erected quite close to the cat flap on the day of the party, and Posy inspected it anxiously from inside the kitchen, while Leo romped wildly inside it. Finally she grew desperate to use her lavatory in the garden, but Leo went and stood outside the cat flap, so that she couldn't pass. We tried to sort it out, but in the end we had other things on our minds, and were relieved, after the party, to see her contentedly sleeping in her basket. Leo, however, was sleeping on the boiler. And there was a certain smell… Posy had had her revenge. She had peed in Leo's basket.

It needed very little invention after this to write *Mog's Bad Thing*. A week or so after the party Leo, rushing without looking as usual, was killed by a car outside our house. We were quite sorry. But Posy bloomed!

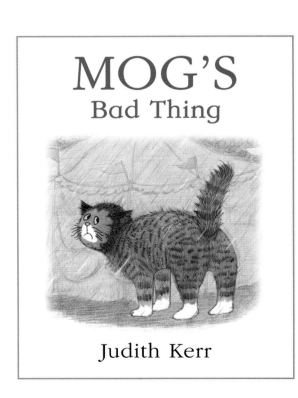

And then Mog did a bad thing.
She did not mean to do it, but she did it.
She did it in Mr Thomas's chair.

My next book was about a goose. I have never particularly wanted to draw geese (though they're quite interesting when you do), but the story was handed to me on a plate and I didn't feel I could waste it. We have a duck pond where I live, and for a while four or five white geese lived on it, but they gradually died or moved away, until there was just one left. He was called Charlie (but in the book I changed it to Katerina). Charlie was known to frequent Barclays bank across the road from the pond. He would wait on the step outside, and sometimes managed to sneak inside. But the thing I first noticed about him was that he used to stand with his beak right up against any shiny car parked nearby and stare and stare at his reflection. He clearly thought it was another goose, and, having lost his brothers and sisters, was lonely.

So I spent a lot of time by the pond drawing him and produced a book called *The Other Goose*. A few years later we came out one morning and found that all the water in the pond had mysteriously drained away in the night, so I did another book called *Goose in a Hole*. It just seemed too good to waste. But I have never felt any great affinity with geese. Not like cats!

It had come out. It had come out! It had come out at last!

Above: from The Other Goose

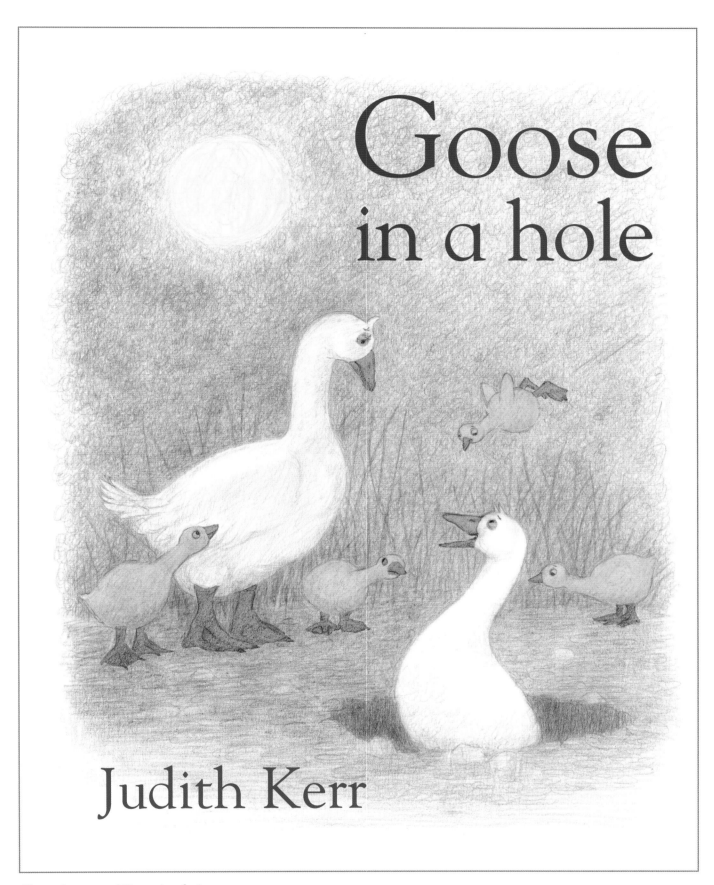

Goose
in a hole

Judith Kerr

Above: the cover of Goose in a hole

MOG
on Fox Night

Judith Kerr

MOG
the Forgetful Cat

Judith Kerr

MOG
and the Baby

Judith Kerr

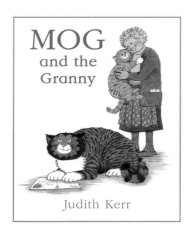

MOG
and the
Granny

Judith Kerr

MOG'S
Amazing
Birthday
Caper

Judith
Kerr

MOG'S
Christmas

Judith Kerr

MOG'S
Bad Thing

Judith Kerr

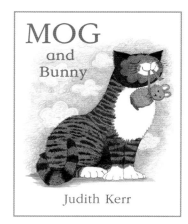

MOG
and
Bunny

Judith Kerr

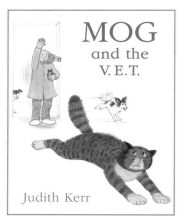

MOG
and the
V.E.T.

Judith Kerr

MOG TIME
6 Stories about Mog

Judith Kerr

Goodbye Mog

Judith Kerr

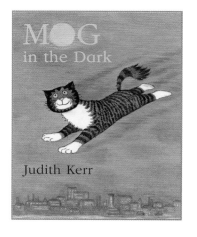

MOG
in the Dark

Judith Kerr

The Mog books had been produced at intervals over so many years that they were all different shapes and sizes, and Ian decided to reprint them in a uniform edition slightly larger than any of the earlier ones, and redesigned all the covers. They look infinitely better than before, and we have kept this larger size for all my books. Unfortunately, it is just too big for me to use my A3 copier, as I had in the past, to transfer a drawing grey with rubbings-out to a clean sheet, and I've had to go back to tracing with my old lightbox. But it was probably getting a bit too mechanical anyway.

So many things have become easier since I started as an illustrator. I use the copier all the time: to record a drawing before I change it, in case it was really better before; to enlarge or reduce parts, sometimes just to see what they would look like. And then there's the Internet! Research was a nightmare before it was invented. I remember searching through the local library for pictures of animals. There was one zoo book for children that was particularly useful, because it not only had good pictures, but it also gave the animals' dimensions, and I stole it. I said I'd lost it and offered to pay for it, but they said children's books did not carry fines, which made it worse. But that book was my bible for years.

Now I just google everything. It's incredible what you can find. For instance, I have successfully googled "open-mouthed tigers". If you went to the zoo instead, first of all, there probably wouldn't be any tigers because, quite rightly, they are no longer confined in cages, and if there were, how long would you have to wait for one to open his mouth? And even if he did, it would probably be at the wrong angle and he'd shut it again very quickly. So I feel very blessed. I don't use a computer to draw on, but obviously for many illustrators they have replaced old-fashioned pencil and paper, and as a result the four artists' suppliers who used to produce my indelible inks have been reduced to one, and the number of colours on offer keeps shrinking. Because of this and perhaps because I've become more tentative in my old age, I have taken to using a lot of crayons on top of slightly diluted inks, which is less bright but more subtle, and also more capable of being altered.

I don't know where the idea of *Goodbye Mog* came from. (The title, of course came from Tom.) But nobody had died. On the contrary, Matthew had got married and was expecting his first child. He had also just won the Whitbread Prize with his novel *English Passengers*, and Tacy was making amazing creatures for the Harry Potter films. It had been a wonderful year. Perhaps it was just that Tom and I were approaching eighty. My father died at that age and my mother had died when she was much younger, but they were both still very much alive to me, so perhaps I was thinking about being remembered after one's death. There was also the fact that over the years our garden had become a veritable cemetery for pets. Not only much-loved cats, but guinea pigs, innumerable hamsters, stick insects and suicidal goldfish were all jostling for position beneath our untended flowerbeds.

For whatever reason, one night I dreamt about my own funeral. It was quite gloomy. Only the children were there, it was cold and dark and pretty depressing, and when it was all over, one of the children said, "What shall we do now?" and the other said, "Let's go to McDonald's." And, ever the yiddisher momma, even in my dream, I thought "Typical! They've hardly got me buried and they go and eat junk food!"

In the morning I thought, of course! This is the way anyone's ghost, especially Mog's, would view the actions of the living, and it became quite easy to write the book. I wasn't sure how the publishers would feel about my killing off a character that had been quite popular, so I didn't tell anyone at first, but in fact they were very supportive. Later I heard from staff in the book shops that the children mostly took Mog's death in their stride, but the mums all wept.

It was greatly helped by Philippa Perry, my publicity consultant, who had the brilliant idea of handling Mog's death as a news item. As a result, death, and how to talk about it to children, became a subject for discussion, and the *Guardian* even wrote Mog a very funny obituary. Philippa also looks after me when I am asked to give talks, so that, after slightly dreading them, I have really come to enjoy them. I have been very lucky to have both her and Ian Craig to help me, and as friends.

Sadly, a few weeks after I had finished off poor Mog, Posy died. I found her in the early hours of a dark winter morning, not in her basket but facing the wall in a corner of the kitchen, so I took her into the living room and sat holding her on my lap, and she purred. After a while Tom woke up and came downstairs, and we took it in turns to hold her. She never stopped purring for two hours. Only for a few minutes at the end she became breathless, and then she died in my arms. She had been our cat for sixteen years, and we did not think we could ever have another.

Opposite and overleaf: from Goodbye Mog

Mog was tired. She was dead tired.
Her head was dead tired.
Her paws were dead tired.
Even her tail was dead tired.
Mog thought, "I want to sleep for ever."
And so she did.
But a little bit of her stayed awake
to see what would happen next.

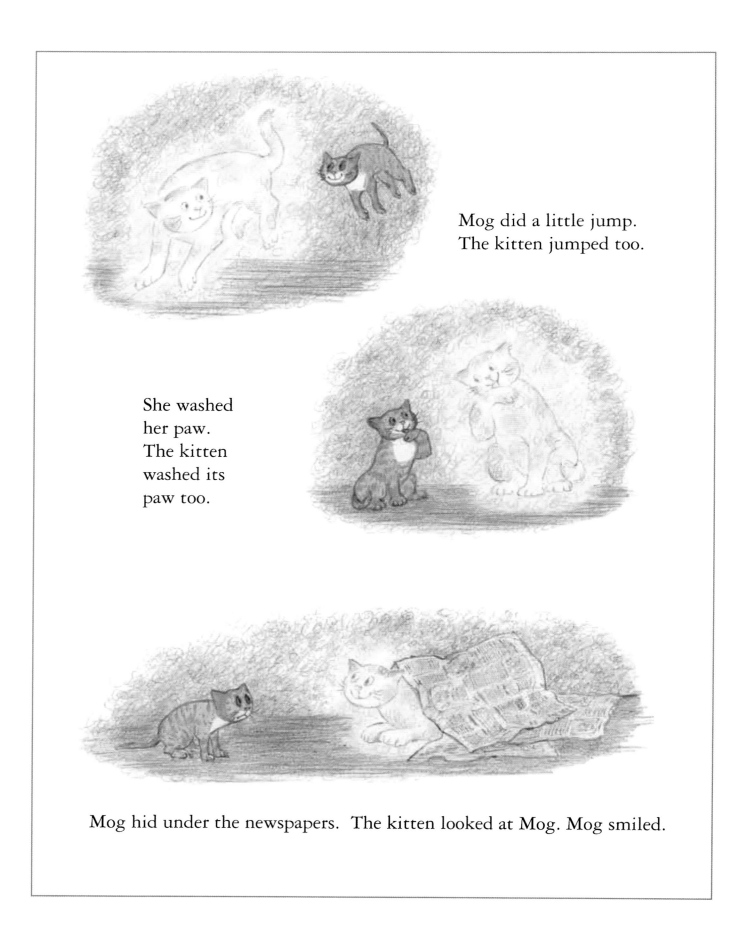

Mog did a little jump.
The kitten jumped too.

She washed
her paw.
The kitten
washed its
paw too.

Mog hid under the newspapers. The kitten looked at Mog. Mog smiled.

The kitten hid too.

The kitten liked playing with the newspapers. Mog thought, "This kitten is not the wrong sort of kitten at all. It just needs a bit of help."

Then one of the bags fell over. All sorts of things fell out.

It was as though *Goodbye Mog* had brought something on.

In 2002 my brother Michael died. We had led very different lives as grown-ups. He had had a huge career in the law as Lord Justice of Appeal, later becoming pre-eminent in the field of International Arbitration. There had been a stormy first marriage followed by a very happy one, dramas…! But we had never lost touch, and we could never forget our close, close childhood and the memory of our parents, and how they got us through a terrifying era.

Then Tom was diagnosed with a stroke. He recovered quickly, but was never quite well again. His last play *Ancient History* about an ex-concentration camp doctor exposed years later in England had gone out just before his seventy-fifth birthday, fifty-five years after the publication of his first short story. Happily, it was beautifully acted and directed, a fitting end to an extraordinary writing career. But he missed writing. Having spent a lifetime using words and inventing stories, he tried several times to start something new, to plan another drama. But he was too tired to complete them. He gradually became more or less housebound, and we spent his last years at home, largely on our own, reading, watching television, and always talking.

Lord Justice of Appeal,
the Rt. Hon. Sir Michael Kerr

Photograph by Matthew Kneale

   We were laughing about the story of a cat we had heard of, which was regularly fed by two different families who both thought it belonged to them, and Tom said, "You *must* do that one!" So that was the beginning of *Twinkles, Arthur and Puss*. I worked on it when I could. He wanted to see how it was getting on, so I used to copy everything I was doing and show it to him. He was hospitalised several times, but in 2004 we managed to celebrate our golden wedding, again with a marquee, but this time without warring cats.

   Tom died in hospital in October 2006. Our children, who had been abroad, rushed home and were able to say goodbye to him, and I was with him at the end. We had been together fifty-four years, but we had never run out of things to talk about.

8

The Last Years

FOR A YEAR OR SO AFTER TOM DIED I couldn't work. It is difficult, after a lifetime of being happily married, to go back to being on one's own. I missed him all the time. But, strangely, having been so happy helped, one thought, "I had all that – how can I complain?" And I found I had joined a club. There were so many other widows, all ready to help. I remember a few months after his death, one of them, a very good friend, took me to see a film. With Tom unwell, I had not been to the cinema for about four years, and I had almost forgotten what it was like. We went to Leicester Square, it was just before Christmas and there were lights everywhere, and people going in and out of shops, and Christmas decorations and street musicians, and I thought, there's all this world that I had almost forgotten! And I thought, one mustn't waste it.

Before I met Tom, like all people who love to draw, I had spent a lot of my time just looking. Together we had so much enjoyed talking that some of the time words, perhaps, took over. Without him, I went back to looking, and I looked and looked. After a while I tried a few drawings. They weren't particularly good because I was so out of practice, but it was a start.

Then I had an idea for a book. Unlike the ideas for my previous books, which had all begun with a plot, this one began with pictures. I wanted to draw an elephant flying through the night, animals doing

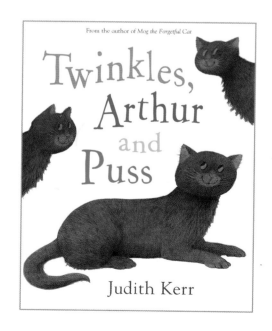

magical things, ridiculous things. I thought of Chagall and dark blue skies, and I had a few lines:

One night in the zoo
The elephant flew
And a lion did tricks
Which astonished a gnu.

Somehow, since there would be very few words it seemed right for them to rhyme. But it was all very vague – too vague. It needed something else, and I couldn't think what. Then, when I was talking to Ian one day, he said, "Why don't you make it into a counting book?" And of course the whole thing immediately fell into shape.

Using rhymes is very interesting. They take one to places one would never normally go to. For instance:

Then a crocodile and a kangaroo
Set off on a bicycle made for two.

I was rather pleased with that. (Until, of course, I had to draw it.) There was a problem with the paper, which had become slightly absorbent of the inks. I tried to make up for it by using lots of crayon on top, but the result is paler than I would have wished. Even so, it sort of worked, and it was something new.

Rough for One Night in the Zoo

Then a crocodile and a kangaroo

Set off on a bicycle made for two,

Earlier that year I had given a talk at the Jewish Book Festival. It was weird, because it was held in a hotel across the road from where we had lived when we had first come to London and where we had been bombed out. There were a lot of questions, so it went on for quite a long time, and I was feeling tired and vaguely haunted by memories at the end, when I was handed a letter with what seemed a wild suggestion.

A theatre producer called Nick Brooke wanted to turn *The Tiger Who Came to Tea* (which takes about three minutes to read) into a one-hour stage play. At first I just thought it was ridiculous, but then I thought, why not, and made an appointment to go and see him. He was clearly very professional, and totally serious. It still seemed a mad idea, but I was having tea with David Wood and his wife Jacqui the following week, and I asked him what he thought. David, of course, has written just about every bit of children's theatre there is, and when he said, rather to my surprise, that he thought he could make it work, we agreed to give it a go.

We met a few times to talk about the sort of thing it should be, and then he wrote it, and there it was – fifty-five minutes of theatre, using the story just as it was, but with songs (composed by himself), and magic and lots of audience participation. He also directed it – it was all done on a shoestring – and when I went to an early rehearsal,

Scenes from the stage version of
The Tiger Who Came to Tea

I was brought up short by the set, which looked exactly like the drawing in the book. There were two young actresses playing Sophie and her mother, and a very good young actor called Alan Atkins playing the tiger, the father and three other characters, and the whole thing just felt effortlessly right. It opened at the Bloomsbury Theatre in August and was an immediate success. It toured on and off and then in 2011 it came to the Vaudeville Theatre in London for the summer season. And in 2012, when it opened at the Lyric, it was nominated for an Olivier award!

It was a huge piece of luck for me. It was wonderful to make contact again with drama, which, since my BBC days, I had always loved. And it is oddly moving to see a theatre full of three-year-olds spellbound by this singing and dancing version of a bedtime story I once told my little daughter so many years ago. I wished Tom could have seen it, but it was nice to remember that David had once acted in one of Tom's plays, and that Tom had told me how very good he had been.

Another very lucky thing that happened was a meeting with Sarah Lawrance. Sarah is the curator of Seven Stories, a fairly new museum of children's books in Newcastle. She was interested in acquiring my original illustrations on loan for the museum. When I began doing picture books, I don't think illustrations were considered art, with the exception of a few classics like Beatrix Potter or Ernest Shepard. In fact, in the sixties illustrators had only just been given royalties rather than a flat buy-out fee. Suddenly, it seemed their work was valued more highly. It had not occurred to me that my drawings would be of interest to anyone except the production people, in case they might be needed for a reprint, and they were all crammed together in my horribly overcrowded and collapsing plan chest. It was very flattering that the museum should want them, and it seemed a good idea for them to be safely stored by people who knew what they were doing.

However, when Philippa first introduced me to Sarah in Durham, where we had gone for me to give a talk, I was not at my best. We had had a fairly disastrous stay with solid rain throughout, and it culminated with my eating a dubious prawn, and a miserable night. The last thing I wanted in the morning was to be driven to Newcastle to look at a museum. However, we had promised Sarah, and so we went.

Newcastle was a revelation. I had never been there, and immediately loved the soaring heights and plunging drops everywhere. You entered the museum which, true to its name, had seven storeys, on what turned out to be the third floor, from which you could go down two storeys to the edge of a deep river bed, or climb up four more to a roof space criss-crossed by huge old wooden beams, which, like much of the rest of the building, were piled with books. There were places for children to read, to dress up and act, to make things, to find out about things. There was space for exhibitions and a children's bookshop, and there were lots of people to help them choose what to do. It was marvellous. My dubious prawn faded from my mind, and I travelled happily back to London with Philippa, knowing that my drawings would not only be well looked after, but stored in a beautiful place.

Some weeks later Sarah and her team came to London and attacked the plan chest, which by then had acquired several immovable drawers. They managed to extract everything and spent some days sorting through it all, and finally carried off everything they needed in a large van. I thought this was the end of it, but to my delight, the following year they set up an exhibition of my work at Seven Stories. Ian, Philippa and I went to the launch, and my brother-in-law Bryan came too. I had had no idea what to expect, but the first thing that caught my eye was a photograph of my father, which I had never seen. They'd found it somewhere on the Internet. There were

my childhood drawings, the books, all sorts of work that I had almost forgotten, and there was also an enormous tiger sitting at a table, so that any child who wished could have tea with him. It was marvellous. The exhibition was a great success and in 2011 it came to London, and I was able to show it to my grandchildren.

Pictures from the exhibition at Seven Stories in Newcastle

By this time I had finished another picture book. This was a bit of an oddity, in that it also had a certain interest for grown-ups – for widows, to be exact. I have always deeply disliked picture books, which, while claiming to be for children, are really self-consciously poetic for grown-ups, and I hope this isn't one of them. It is about a widow who fantasises about wild adventures with her husband in heaven, and at least it is quite funny. So far at least some children seem to like it too. At the time of writing it has only just come out in paperback, and it will be interesting to see how it does.

Roughs for **My Henry**

Rough for the cover of **My Henry**

Judith Kerr
MY HENRY

The hardback cover

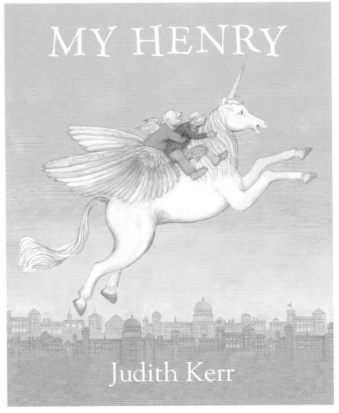

Drawing for the cover of **My Henry**

MY HENRY

Judith Kerr

The paperback cover

MY HENRY

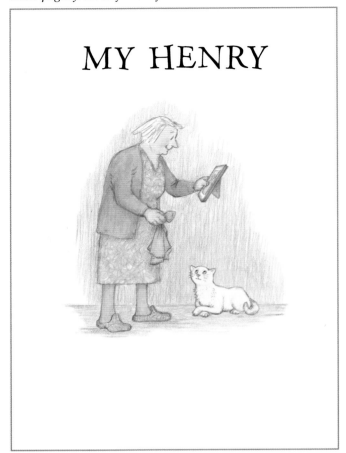

They think I'm sitting in this chair
Just waiting for my tea.

In fact, I'm flying through the air
With Henry holding me.

My Henry died and went to heaven,
But now he's got his wings
They let him out from four till seven
And we do all sorts of things.

...that I am chatting with the Sphinx
Who's asked us out to Sunday drinks
With several friends in tow.

It's things we've never tried before
That are the greatest fun,
Like riding on a dinosaur,
Which I had never done.

Title page for The Great Granny Gang

My most recent picture book is called *The Great Granny Gang*. Old ladies again, I am afraid, but then I know so many of them, and they are really very interesting to draw. The grannies are all remarkably energetic for their age and end up defeating a gang of hoodies. It is again in rhyme and not particularly realistic. I have dedicated it to some of my friends.

And that's it, really. All being well, by the time this autobiography is published I shall be ninety. It has been an amazingly full and happy life, but it could so easily not have been so. If it hadn't been for my parents' foresight, if this country hadn't given us shelter, and if sixty years ago I hadn't gone to lunch in the BBC canteen…!

Portrait by Tacy Kneale

I owe thanks to a lot of people, from the man who bent the rules to give me a scholarship, to my publishers who took a chance on my first book and have supported me ever since. I have a new cat called Katinka. She is white, but with a tabby tail, and most mornings when I draw back the curtains I find that she has climbed up the creeper and is sitting on the windowsill to greet me. We do all right together.

Once, as a teenager talking to my father, I said that perhaps I might like to do illustration one day, and he said, "You'll have to work very hard, because they are very good at it in this country." He was right. They are. I think I am very lucky to have joined them.

This book is dedicated to
the one and a half million Jewish children
who didn't have my luck,
and all the pictures they might
have painted.

Chronology

1923	June 14	Anna Judith Gertrud Helene Kerr born in Berlin
1933	March	The Kerr family flee to Switzerland Hitler seizes power
	Spring	Judith's father Alfred Kerr's books are publicly burned by the Nazis. He is deprived of his German nationality and a price is put on his head.
	December	The family move to Paris
1936	March	The family move to London
1939	September 3	Outbreak of the Second World War
1940	May	Judith's brother Michael is interned on the Isle of Man
	October	The family are bombed out Judith starts work for the Hon. Mrs Gamage
1941	Spring	London art schools reopen evening classes
1942		Michael joins the RAF
1945	May 8	End of the War in Europe
	September	Awarded a scholarship at the Central School of Art and Crafts and begins a part-time job in a textile studio
1947	January	The family become naturalised British subjects Judith's mother Julia Kerr starts work for the Americans in occupied Germany
1948	July	Judith fails diploma in book illustration
	October	Father dies in Hamburg
1948 – 1952		Teaching art in various schools
1952	February	Judith and Tom meet for the first time Judith becomes a reader of unsolicited plays for BBC television
1953	July	*The Quatermass Experiment* broadcast by the BBC Judith is promoted to reader of drama at BBC
1954	May 8	Judith and Tom are married Tom's adaptation of George Orwell's *1984* is broadcast
1955		*Quatermass II* broadcast
1956		Judith becomes a BBC scriptwriter Mother attempts suicide in Berlin
1957		*Huntingtower* broadcast
1958	January 3	Tacy Deborah Kneale born
		Look Back in Anger film premiere
	December	*Quatermass and the Pit* broadcast
1960		*The Entertainer* film premiere
	November 24	Matthew Nicholas Kerr Kneale born
1961		Michael becomes a QC
1962		Move to Barnes
1963		*The Road* broadcast
1965		Mother dies in Berlin
1968		*The Year of the Sex Olympics* broadcast
		The Tiger Who Came to Tea published

1969	Tom writes *Tai Pan* script in Rome		1996	**Mog and the V.E.T.** published
1970	*Wine of India* broadcast **Mog the Forgetful Cat** published		1997	*Wo Liegt Berlin?* by Alfred Kerr becomes a bestseller in Germany
1971	**When Hitler Stole Pink Rabbit** published		1998	Alfred Kerr Darsteller Preis established in Berlin
1972	*The Stone Tape* broadcast **When Willy Went to the Wedding** published		1998	*Ancient History* broadcast **Birdie Halleluyah!** published
1974	Visit Germany to be awarded the German Youth Book Prize		2000	Matthew marries Shannon Russell Tacy makes creatures for *Harry Potter* films **Mog's Bad Thing** published
1975	**The Other Way Round** published (later called **Bombs on Aunt Dainty**)		2001	Matthew wins the Whitbread Award Birth of grandson Alexander Dante Kerr Russell Kneale **The Other Goose** published
1976	**Mog's Christmas** published			
1978	**A Small Person Far Away** published			
1979	*Quatermass* broadcast		2002	Michael dies **Goodbye Mog** published
1980	**Mog and the Baby** published		2003	Birth of granddaughter Tatiana Ella Russell Kneale
1981	Michael becomes Lord Justice of Appeal			
1982	To Japan to visit Matthew To LA. Tom scripts *Halloween III*		2005	**Goose in a Hole** published
1983	Tom takes his name off *Halloween III* **Mog in the Dark** published		2006	Judith receives the J. M. Barrie Award October 29 Tom dies
1984	**Mog and Me** published		2007	**Twinkles, Arthur and Puss** published
1985	**Mog's Family of Cats** published		2008	Tacy has an exhibition of paintings with Colin Beagley **The Tiger Who Came to Tea** adapted for the stage
1986	**Mog's ABC** published			
1988	Matthew wins the Somerset Maugham Award **Mog and Bunny** published		2009	Seven Stories take over original art work Exhibition in Newcastle Tacy has a second exhibition of paintings with Colin Beagley **One Night in the Zoo** published
1989	Tom's TV adaptation of Susan Hill's *The Woman in Black* broadcast			
1991	Tom's TV adaptation of Kingsley Amis's *Stanley and the Women* broadcast **Mog and Barnaby** published		2011	Seven Stories exhibition at V & A Museum of Childhood, Bethnal Green, London **My Henry** published
1992	Matthew wins John Llewellyn Rhys prize **How Mrs Monkey Missed the Ark** published		2012	Judith receives an OBE for services to children's literature and Holocaust education **The Great Granny Gang** published Tacy's third exhibition of paintings with Colin Beagley
1993	**Mog on Fox Night** published The Judith Kerr School opens in Berlin			
1994	**Mog in the Garden** and **Mog's Kittens** published			
1995	**Mog and the Granny** published			

Acknowledgements:

I owe thanks to: Ian Craig, Sally Gritten, HarperCollins, Sarah Lawrance, Helen Mackenzie Smith, Ann-Janine Murtagh, Gail Penston, Philippa Perry, Mark Le Fanu and The Society of Authors, James Stevens and David Wood.

The author and publishers wish to thank the following for their kind permission to reproduce works in their collections and to permit the inclusion of copyright material:

Photograph of Bryan Kneale, p61 copyright © Harry Borden
Photograph of Alfie Burke, p84 copyright © Fremantle Media Ltd / Rex Features
Photographs of David Wood's stage adaptation of *The Tiger Who Came to Tea*, pp162-3, copyright © Bob Workman
Photographs of *From The Tiger Who Came to Tea to Mog & Pink Rabbit; A Judith Kerr Retrospective Exhibition*, p165 by courtesy of Seven Stories

Every reasonable effort has been made to contact copyright holders of material reproduced in this book, but if any have been inadvertently overlooked the publishers would be glad to hear from them and to make good in future editions any omissions brought to their attention.

Seven Stories, The National Centre for Children's Books, in Newcastle upon Tyne, exists to preserve, celebrate, and share the wonderful work of Britain's writers and illustrators for children. As part of the Seven Stories Collection, Judith's archive is held alongside manuscripts and artwork by many leading writers and illustrators, from the 1930s to the present day. For full details of the current programme and visitor information, see our website: www.sevenstories.org.uk. To view the archive, please email collections@sevenstories.org.uk, preferably at least two weeks before your visit. Information about Judith's archive, and the rest of the Seven Stories Collection, can be found at www.sevenstories.org.uk/collection.